About the Book

Jimmy Connors has been called Mouth, the bad boy of tennis—mean, crude, a spoiled brat. Sometimes, indeed, it seems his fame comes from his unpopular behavior on the courts rather than from being the greatest tennis player of his time. In this absorbing biography author Francene Sabin shows that Connors is—like most people—a mixture in his personality. She offers the reader a close look at a great athlete in both his public and his personal life.

by Francene Sabin

Jimmy Connors

KING OF THE COURTS

G. P. Putnam's Sons, New York

Photo Credit
UCLA pp. 84, 86, 87
UPI pp. 85, 88, 89

Copyright © **1978 by Francene Sabin**
All rights reserved. Published simultaneously in Canada by
Longman Canada Limited, Toronto. Printed in the United
States of America   10 up

Library of Congress Cataloging in Publication Data
Sabin, Francene. Jimmy Connors, king of the courts.
(Putnam sports shelf) Includes index. SUMMARY: High-
lights the life of champion Jimmy Connors on and off the
tennis courts. 1. Connors, Jimmy, 1952-   —Juvenile
literature. 2. Tennis players—United States—Biography—
Juvenile literature. [1. Connors, Jimmy, 1952- 2. Tennis
players] I. Title. GV994.C66S22   796.34′2′0924 [B] [92]
77-11688 ISBN 0-399-61115-0

For my brother, Bert

Contents

Introduction   11

1   A Wonderful Wimbledon Win   13

2   In the Beginning   25

3   Jimmy the Giant Killer   39

4   The Master Touch   51

5   Something Money Can't Buy   60

6   More Firsts for Jimmy   73

7   Jimmy and Chris and the Sophomore Slump   92

8   ''The Mean Machine''   103

9   Jimmy Connors vs. the World   116

10   The Match of the Century   126

11   The New Jimmy Connors   136

12   No. One in the World   145

Index   157

Acknowledgments

The author wishes to express gratitude to Lee Greene, Charlie Mercer, and her devoted tennis partner, Lou Sabin.

Introduction

He was called Mouth, the bad boy of tennis, mean, crude, a spoiled brat. In fact, it often seemed as if Jimmy Connors' fame came from his unpopular behavior rather than from being the greatest tennis player of his time. Connors was like most people, a mixture of good qualities and bad. But Jimmy's nicer side was usually ignored.

There was the Jimmy Connors who always took the trouble to speak to young, unknown players at tournaments; who would congratulate them on wins and console them on losses. Most tennis stars snubbed everyone except other stars. Not Jimmy. But that side of him was seldom written about.

Then there were the kids who begged for autographs or who hung around tournaments, hoping for a glimpse of the action and their heroes. Jimmy always had time for autographs—even if fifty youngsters wanted them. And he was the one player who would take a bunch of kids through the gates to watch the matches. Since they loved tennis so much, he'd be their ticket to the arena.

And there was the time Connors was in Las Vegas to play a challenge match against Rod Laver. Sightseeing a few nights before the match, Jimmy wandered through a gambling casino. There, at the slot machines, was an elderly woman who had just hit the jackpot. A pile of silver dollars tumbled out of the machine. Jimmy helped her pick them off the floor and put them into her purse. Then, because she was afraid to walk to her hotel room alone with so much money, Jimmy escorted her. At her door the woman tried to give him a dollar tip for his kindness. Jimmy didn't want to accept it, but she insisted, telling him that it might be the start of *his* fortune. She hadn't recognized the kind young man, who had earned almost $300,000 the year before, and Jimmy was too polite to say something which might embarrass her.

Obviously, Jimmy Connors was a much more complex human being than most people were led to believe. How he came to be a star and the reasons for his on-and-off court behavior make a fascinating story. Here, then, is Jimmy Connors, King of the Courts.

1

A Wonderful Wimbledon Win

Saturday, July 6, 1974. The weather had been terrible all week, and the grass at Wimbledon, England's famous tennis club, was slick and dangerous. The arena was jammed with people lucky enough to have tickets to the match of matches—the men's final. In the dressing room under the stands, two players waited like tigers, eager to be uncaged.

For twenty-one-year-old Jimmy Connors, the biggest test of his life was moments away. He would be facing Ken Rosewall, the thirty-nine-year-old Australian star who was almost a tennis legend. The crowd would be on Rosewall's side, rooting for the "old man" in what might be his last chance at the crown. The whole world would be watching—the crowd around Centre Court and millions on television—as the two players competed for the most coveted title in tennis.

It was down to this for Connors: Win three sets and be the king of the sport; lose and be just another also-ran. Second-place finishers are seldom remembered.

In the arena the spectators rose to their feet. The Duke of Kent, representing Her Majesty Queen Elizabeth II, entered the royal box. Only now could play begin. There was an instant of noise and flurry, then silence as every head turned to watch as the players emerged from beneath the stands and made the traditional bows to the royal family. Ritual observed, Jimmy Connors and Ken Rosewall took their places at opposite ends of the court. The final match was ready to begin. . . .

Reaching the finals hadn't been easy for Jimmy. There had been times when it looked as if he would never make it. In his second-round match against Phil Dent of Australia, Connors had been two points away from defeat. He had dropped the first set, 5–7, won the second, 6–3, lost the third, 3–6, and tied it up by taking the fourth set, 6–3. But the fifth set was going very badly for Jimmy, with Dent leading, six games to five, and ahead, 30–0, in the twelfth game. Hanging on the rim of defeat, Connors fought back heroically, taking the set, 10–8, to win the match.

Even though he had come through in the clutch, having to battle his way through five sets against Dent had shaken the young American. When a reporter asked him how he felt after the match, Jimmy had a one-word answer: "overseeded." Clearly, the narrow brush with defeat had made a deep impression on him.

Wimbledon, where the world's best compete to crown the best of the best, was grueling, gritty tennis from start to finish. This fact became obvious again to Jimmy when, after two fairly easy wins, he faced Jan Kodes in the quarterfinals. Kodes, the 1973 Wimbledon champ, had the knack of turning an almost sure loss into a comeback victory. And here, after the fourth set against Connors, it seemed about to happen again.

Jimmy was leading two sets to one (3–6, 6–3, 6–3) and was up, 6–5, in the fourth. Then Kodes rallied strongly to win it, 8–6. As they went into the fifth set, the odds appeared to be in favor of the Czechoslovakian. Not only had he clinched the fourth set, but he had done it with two games in which Connors had scored no points! The momentum definitely was with Kodes.

Even so, the boy from Belleville, Illinois, wasn't about to throw in the towel. His nerves might be tingling, but he wasn't a quitter. As his mother, his fiancée, and his manager watched in fascinated silence, Jimmy dug down and began slamming his way back. His ground strokes skimmed over the net to wherever Kodes wasn't. Power and pinpoint accuracy were doing the job for him, and Kodes was staggering as Jimmy's volleys boomed with murderous force. Connors wrapped up the fifth set, 6–3, solidly earning his berth in the semifinals.

But the closer he got to the big match, the greater the tension grew. And this match, the semi, was one away from the big one. Jimmy's nerves were almost screaming, and in the first set against Dick Stockton, he couldn't get his game together. The two-handed backhand shots, for which he was famous, weren't landing right. Stockton, an unseeded player from New York, was moving Connors all over the court, keeping the pressure on. Jimmy needed to settle down, but the pace was too fast. This was slam-bang tennis—no long rallies, no time for strategy. Too soon Stockton had the lead, and the crowd was roaring. And too soon the first set was over, and Jimmy's worst fears were coming true. He had lost it, 4–6.

As the second set got under way, Connors still looked rocky, and he managed to take only one of the first three games. Then, amazingly, he turned things around.

In the stands, Chris Evert, Jimmy's fiancée, was leaving her seat. She had to get ready for the women's finals. Perhaps it was seeing her go—with the reminder that it was possible for them to make sports history together—that brought back Connors' form. Or maybe, at precisely that moment, he recaptured the total concentration of the true superathlete.

Whatever the reason, Connors was suddenly transformed into a giant on the smooth grass court. He reeled off eight straight games, his stunning comeback throwing Stockton on the defensive. The second set was 6–2, Connors. The third set was Connors, 6–3. The fourth set was 6–4, Connors. The winner was Jimmy Connors, and it was a *big* win.

As soon as the match was over, a weary Dick Stockton said, "Playing Connors is like fighting Joe Frazier. The guy's always coming at you. He never lets up."

Meanwhile, a relieved Jimmy, still wearing his sweat-soaked tennis whites, rushed to Centre Court to watch Chris Evert become the women's champion. Friday had been a busy day for the two young stars.

Now it was Saturday, and a crucial test faced Jimmy. Everything else in the world faded away as he focused his mind on the strategy he had to use against Ken Rosewall. The idea was to start slowly, stay back, and give himself the advantage of time. The contest pitted youth against age, and the strong, five-foot-ten-inch, twenty-one-year-old Jimmy had the edge that came with springy legs and the stamina of a young body. Without a doubt, time was an ally of Jimmy.

Years of practice and experience, coupled with his rabbit-quick speed, had taught Jimmy what kind of game worked best for him. He would attack the ball, catching a return or a serve on the rise, and whip it back. The Australian—a canny, courtwise veteran—had to be kept on the defensive, had to be kept moving. If Jimmy could make Rosewall play the game the Connors way . . . If he could maintain strict concentration, never easing up in mind or body . . . If. . . .

It was Rosewall's service as the match opened

under a sunny English sky. Jimmy smoothed back his brown hair and crouched low, like a hungry cat eyeing a mouse, and waited. Rosewall's first serve came over the net, and it was clear to anyone familiar with Jimmy's style that he was holding back a bit, wisely collecting significant facts and sorting them out in his mind. It would add up very soon—the way the ball was acting in the air, the effect of the wind, the way the ball bounced off the grass, the tactics Rosewall was using.

Rosewall showed no such patience. He was playing in his fourth Wimbledon final, and that gave him confidence. He also knew he couldn't afford to hold back, because time was as much his enemy as it was Jimmy's ally. So he hit the ball with everything he had and took the first game of the first set.

The audience cheered. Rosewall was the sentimental favorite, while Connors was that brash kid from America who didn't always have the best tennis manners. "I had about eight fans there, I think," Connors said after the match. But even though he might have liked having a larger rooting section, he wouldn't let anyone or anything throw him off his game.

Connors' service in the second game had the impact of a wrecking ball. Rosewall was shaken by blow after blow! How do you stop the kid? his expression seemed to be asking.

The score went to 1–1, and the arena fell silent. It was Rosewall's service now, and Jimmy bent into his swaying crouch. To one sportswriter he looked like "an alert cobra." The serve spun across the net, and almost immediately the American sizzled it back. Rosewall answered ably, but Jimmy was there, ready to strike. His forehand passing shot, carrying the force of his whole body behind it, made the score 0–15, Connors. On the next serve a Connors smash upped his lead to 0–30. Then a backhand (Jimmy's two-handed doomsday weapon) took the game to 0–40. Then a spinning ground stroke to Kenny's backhand finished it. The American's thunderbolts had broken Rosewall's serve.

In the twenty-one minutes of the entire first set—a grueling one for the Australian—Rosewall won only the first game. The rest, in merciless succession, were Jimmy's The score: 6–1.

The first four games of the second set flew by just as swiftly, with Connors surging ahead, 4–0. The match was turning into a massacre. Still, Rosewall's faithful fans rooted and hoped. The Aussie elder statesman had been down two sets in his semifinal match with Stan Smith and had come back to win it. Maybe he could do it again.

Rosewall tried. Oh, how he tried! Six times the score went to deuce, only to end in favor of Connors. Rosewall's backhand, normally a stroke of power and infinite precision, was falling apart, unraveled by Jimmy's forceful, brilliant play.

As Connors set to serve, a fan called out desperately to Rosewall, "Give it a go!" The old master showed no sign that he heard. Neither did Jimmy, but it did get through to him. And oddly, it affected his play. Even though he was in command of the match, he suddenly began to look uncertain—and play that way. He hit the ball into the net more than once and double-faulted to lose the game. "Rosewall didn't win the game," said an observer, "so much as Connors lost it." But that one game was all Ken was going to get from Jimmy. Connors regrouped and wrapped up the set, 6–1, in thirty-two minutes.

The American took the first game of the third set, breaking Rosewall's serve again. Then, with a flicker of the style that had made him a champion for twenty years, Ken broke Jimmy's serve to knot the set at 1–all. Encouraged, Rosewall went on to hold his own serve and go up, 2–1. Now the crucial game was coming up. If he could break Connors' serve once more, the old man would have a chance to turn things around. He might even shake Connors' confidence. But the Aussie also knew that if he didn't do it now, it would be all over but the mopping up.

A heavy hush enveloped the crowd. Only the sound of the colorful flags snapping in the breeze could be heard in the arena. The last thing Rosewall's tight-lipped fans wanted was to interrupt their favorite's ministreak in any way.

Connors bounced the ball a few times, swaying back and forth in rhythm with the bounce. Then he squinted over the net like a pitcher reading his catcher's signs. Rosewall waited tensely for the serve, his grip tightening on the racket handle. At last the ball came humming at him, and he sprang to meet it. . . .

The action was fast and deadly and even, with both players refusing to give an inch. The score swung back and forth, reaching 30–30. Then, on the strength of a zinging Rosewall backhand that burst right at Connors' feet, it was 30–40. One more point, and the Australian would clinch another game.

But the American wouldn't cooperate and took the game to deuce. Another point for Rosewall . . . back again to deuce. . . .

The usually reserved British fans let loose a round of clapping that sounded like thunder. And Rosewall, responding, slammed a backhand volley that gave him advantage for the second time.

Before Jimmy set for his next serve, he paced back and forth along the baseline, adjusting his racket strings. He had to take the lead; he had to play *his* game. Let Rosewall get this one, and the psychological edge might be too much to overcome. As Jimmy paced and thought, the fans started showing their impatience. But he wouldn't be rushed. Not now.

This was the time, if ever there was one, for Jimmy to think about the advice of his coach, Pancho Segura. Segura, a wily old pro, had spent years on tour with Rosewall and had developed a line of strategy. As Connors explained after the match,

"Pancho said, 'Stay away from the net and rally,' so I did. He also said, 'Get every return into play, and take the ball on the rise,' so I did."

Whatever flood of thoughts poured through Jimmy's mind, his pre-serve pause worked. He brought the game back to deuce, then went on to take it. That evened the score at 2–2. In the next four games both competitors held their service, bringing the tally to 4–4. Nevertheless, with each moment the end became clearer. The reason was obvious for everyone witnessing the action: Time was beginning to tell.

Rosewall, the old warrior, was weary. His steps were slowing; the perspiration was streaking his sunburned face, making it look old and pained. His nickname on the international tennis circuit had always been Muscles, in tribute to his great strength. At this moment, though, he was just a short, valiant middle-aged man. And as expected, in the ninth game of the third set, Connors—the youngster with enough energy to go on another couple of hours—broke Rosewall's service and made it 5–4.

Jimmy took over the serve and charged in for the kill. "Boom! Boom! Boom! I got it to forty-love," he later said of the game. Then the serve for match point, and Rosewall, clinging to hope like a drowning man grasping at a lifeline, took the point: 40–15. Again, Connors' cannonball serve. Again Rosewall held on to survive: 40–30.

As Jimmy prepared to serve match point for the

third time, even the wind whipping the flags around seemed to hold its breath. He served—a fault—prolonging the agony of tension already at the breaking point. Then, at last, the second serve blurred into Rosewall's court, and the Australian's backhand return blipped softly into the net: 6–4. Jimmy Connors was the king of Wimbledon, and it had taken him only 93 nerve-racking minutes to do it.

The fans applauded graciously. But Jimmy couldn't contain his emotions. He threw his racket into the air with joy and leaped over the net to shake hands with Ken Rosewall.

Newsmen from all over the world surged onto the court to hear the victor's words and photograph his happy grin. All of a sudden, the enormity of his achievement engulfed the twenty-one-year-old, and he began to cry. This was the crest of the hill he had started climbing when he was a small child. This was what tennis was all about—championship.

The Duke of Kent made his way onto Centre Court. There he presented Jimmy the winner's check of $24,000 and the impressive, huge gold cup given only to Wimbledon winners. Jimmy gazed at it through teary eyes, kissed it, and lofted it over his head. Not until later, when his storm of emotion had calmed, could Jimmy talk about his thoughts and feelings.

"This was something I dreamed of," he said, "since I was six years old. I was in tears at the umpire's stand after the match because I thought, this is perhaps the only time in my life that I shall be in such a position.

"After I made it to the finals," Jimmy remembered, "I watched Chrissie play, and she won. That was one half, one half of the double, and then I had to play. But, you know, I don't think that we thought we'd both win it this year. I only really knew I'd won when he hit his backhand return into the net at match point."

Pancho Segura, as happy as if he had just taken the title himself, said, "Jimmy is a real killer with the heart of a lion. He has a great mental approach and pride. He gets steamed up one hundred percent. He can't stand losing." He paused, then went on, "Jimmy has the best service of anyone in the game. He is tough not only in any match, but in any situation, too. In the final, Jimmy must have known that almost everyone was willing his opponent to win."

Yes, Connors knew how the Wimbledon fans felt about Rosewall and was philosophical about it. "I knew he was the sentimental favorite," Jimmy said modestly. "Maybe someday I'll be a sentimental favorite. But I may never do it again. I'm no Newcombe or Laver. I never played better tennis in my life."

2

In the Beginning

It was a warm, clear day early in the spring of 1955. A slim young woman walked out onto a backyard tennis court in East St. Louis, Illinois. She was followed by two very small boys. "Okay, Johnny and Jimmy," she said to them. "You two try to hit the balls Mommy throws."

The two sneaker-clad preschoolers, holding sawed-off tennis rackets, took their places. Johnny, aged four, managed to hit a few of the tennis balls his mother bounced to him. Two-and-a-half-year-old Jimmy copied whatever his bigger brother did. If Johnny could do it, little Jimmy wanted to do it, too.

"Everything Jimmy did, he tried to excel at," his father said years later. "He tried to match Johnny stride for stride, and I still think that's what gave him his competitive drive and desire."

Every day, except when it was raining, the boys went out to their court to play this new game their mother liked so much. Too small and weak to manage a backhand shot with one hand, they used two hands to hold the racket. Some tennis coaches frowned on this unorthodox technique, but not Gloria Connors. She knew that the important thing was for her sons to enjoy themselves and to enjoy some success at the game. If a one-handed backhand was too difficult and she still insisted that it was the only way, they might become discouraged with the sport. Or they might shy away from all backhand strokes. In either case, that was not the way to shape her boys into tennis champions—and that was something she wanted more than anything else.

Mrs. Connors, an excellent tennis player in her youth, had quit the tournament circuit when she had gotten married. Even so, she had never stopped loving the game and wanting to be part of it. To her, tennis was more than a sport. It was a way of life. Tennis meant the outdoors, fresh air, clean living, dedication, and good health. What could be better than an activity like that for two young boys?

Tennis was also a family tradition for Gloria Connors. Her mother, Bertha Thompson, had been a top Midwestern player many years before. When Gloria herself had been five years old, her mother had taught her to play the game. And Mrs. Thompson had remained her coach until Gloria had given up the sport at the age of nineteen. Now it was time to pass the tradition on to the next generation: Johnny and Jimmy Connors.

Some people have criticized Gloria Connors, accusing her of having forced her sons into tennis. But that is unfair. Just as a doctor's child is often encouraged to become a doctor, and a businessman's child is groomed for a business career, so it is in sports. Jim Evert, father of Chris Evert, was a tennis pro who taught all his children to play when they were very small. In that family, of three girls and two boys, only the girls had the desire and drive to stick with the sport. Without a father coaching and guiding her, Chris Evert might never have become a tennis champion.

This sort of family tradition in sports is not restricted to tennis, as most sports fans know. Press Maravich, a basketball star and coach, purposely trained his son Pete to be a brilliant basketball player. Together, throughout Pete's childhood, they worked on all the skills he would need to develop into a superstar on the court. And Pete Rose, of baseball fame, was molded by a father who had been an all-round athlete in his own youth and who clearly wanted his son to be a major leaguer in at least one sport.

The parent-child connection in athletics is really not unusual at all. There are Gordie Howe and his three sons playing together for the same hockey team; Gladys Heldman and her daughter Julie both involved in pro tennis; Kyle Rote, Sr., in football and Kyle, Jr., in soccer; baseball's Yogi Berra and his sons Dale and Larry, who went into football . . . the list is almost endless.

The only difference between all these and the Connors story is that Jimmy became a star under the guidance of two women, his mother and grandmother. But you can bet that the name Connors would have been high in tennis rankings whether Gloria had sons or daughters. This was the way she was going to bring up her children because this was what she believed was the best way. The boys would be given every opportunity in the sport, right from the beginning. The rest would be up to them.

Johnny liked practicing on the family courts, but Jimmy *loved* it. He never could get enough playing time. He wanted to run and hit the ball from sunrise to sunset. This willing attitude made Gloria Connors very happy, though she sometimes worried about so much intensity from such a little guy. When it came to tennis, Jimmy would do whatever his mother told him. "He *never* resisted," Mrs. Connors said. "As a matter of fact, all through his life I often had to stop him. That was always my big concern—I was afraid he'd overplay, that he'd burn himself out."

But Jimmy simply wanted to play tennis, the way some boys love to read or play a musical instrument. Nothing else mattered so much to him. Soon it was more than Gloria Connors could manage by herself, and her mother, Bertha Thompson, began to help with instruction and coaching. Mrs. Thompson was delighted with the ability of her grandsons and their eagerness to be taught. And they were just as delighted at having a grandma who was so good at sports. To Jimmy and Johnny she was much more than a grandmother; she was a pal, a teacher, another mother.

One day the boys made an announcement. As always, they said, Gloria Connors would be Mom. From now on, however, Bertha Thompson would be Two-Moms. It was their way of confirming the specialness of their family group and the enjoyment they found in being part of it.

They made quite a foursome—Mom, Two-Moms, Johnny, and Jimmy. Aside from the hours spent in school (the boys attended St. Philip School, run by their local parish in East St. Louis), all attention was directed to sports. The two women were ready and waiting when the boys dashed home every afternoon. There was just time to drop their books, have a snack, change into tennis clothes, and they were ready to play. That's when the work would begin.

To keep the boys from getting bored, practice sessions were different from day to day. One afternoon they might work on ground strokes, another on serves, another on volleys. Part of the time the boys might play together against Mom and Two-Moms or on a doubles team of one adult and one child against the other pair. But the boys found the most fun and excitement came when they played a singles match against each other. That was also when their competitiveness came through. Johnny, the elder, fought to stay on top. Jimmy ached to outdo his big brother.

There were some days when the matches were so heated that people passing by would stop to watch. Word began to spread in East St. Louis that, if you wanted to see some rough, tough tennis, get over to Sixty-eight and State and catch the Connors family in action. And, sure enough, many of the afternoon practice matches were carried on in front of crowds of onlookers.

James Connors, Sr., father of the two tiny tennis prodigies, felt both pride and amazement at what was happening. As a youth he had been very athletic himself—playing golf, tennis, and baseball and riding horses—and he was pleased at the idea that his own boys were really fine athletes. He sometimes wished that he had more time to give them, but his job as manager of the toll bridge that connects Illinois with Missouri kept Mr. Connors from taking an active part in his sons' development. Still, he was glad that his wife and her mother had the time and the ability to help the boys.

Though at first Johnny seemed to have more tennis talent than Jimmy, Mr. Connors always maintained that his younger son would be the one to go all the way. "Jimmy worked so hard," the proud father said, "it became an obsession. He had an added spark."

Despite the fact that Johnny was beating his little brother at the sport, he could foresee that the situation was bound to change. "He'd play tennis," Johnny said of Jimmy, "come home and go to bed and dream tennis, and then have tennis for breakfast. That's all he thought about."

There was no need to push or coax Jimmy—he'd do anything to better his game. If Mom and Two-Moms suggested roadwork to strengthen his legs, Jimmy would willingly run to exhaustion. When they added rope skipping to the training program, he was equally enthusiastic, trying to do it 10,000 times without missing. For him, it was like homework for a dedicated scholar.

Practice sessions on the court were the best part of Jimmy's day. "We put in maybe forty-five minutes at a time," Jimmy recalled, "tough workouts, then rest. I loved it. They always made me stop at the 'eager' stage where I couldn't wait to start again. People have criticized my mom for trying to make me what she wasn't, but these people don't realize this is what I always wanted. Tennis was *my* choice, *my* life. I never had time for friends or anything else. I didn't even know anybody in school, I was too busy. I used to leave class every day at noon to practice tennis."

And Gloria Connors remembered those years in the same way. "He was nothing but a delight and a pleasure to work with," she said of young Jimmy. "Nothing was too much. If I had told him he had to stand on his head to hit the ball, he'd have done it! He always had the talent; he was always outstanding, even as a small boy."

To spice up life with some variety and to keep tennis from becoming the *only* thing, the Connors encouraged other sports. The boys played basketball, soccer, and baseball, rode horses, and swam—everything the other kids in the neighborhood were doing. To Jimmy, however, that part of life didn't count nearly as much as playing tennis and playing it well.

"I had a great childhood," Jimmy said, "with go-carts and horses and everything. But when it came to playing something else with the kids or working on tennis with Mom, I always chose tennis. I wanted to be the best."

Very early there was no denying that Jimmy Connors was a heck of a tennis player. As an age-group competitor, he was well known in the Midwest by the time he was ten years old. And even then the style that would carry him to the peak on the international circuit was well established. There were those long, arrow-sharp ground strokes, the power-packed two-handed backhand shots, and his never-say-die grittiness. It didn't matter that Jimmy was always small for his age; he refused to let that discourage him. If anything, it was just another challenge to meet and defeat. No matter how much bigger his opponent might be, Jimmy more than made up the difference by digging down that much deeper, playing that much harder.

Butch Buchholz, a former pro from St. Louis, knew the young Jimmy Connors and admired the boy's "class" as a player. "As a young guy," Buchholz said, "Jimmy really understood the court very well.

He really knew how to win a point. He had some problems with his game—he didn't serve that well, didn't volley that well—but he had the ground strokes. And he was totally dedicated as a player, even as a little guy.''

Buchholz didn't agree in the least with the accusations that Jimmy was forced by his family to be a tennis player. "Nine out of ten kids would have rebelled, but Jimmy ate it up, he enjoyed it," Buchholz declared, going on to say that many of the mean remarks made about Jimmy sprang from the envy of others. It's something that most champions have to live with.

Jimmy heard the criticisms, but he wasn't on the tennis court to win popularity contests—just the matches. He didn't care whether his opponents liked him or not. He didn't even think about it. His mind was filled with thoughts of tennis, and very little else could compete with that.

As Buchholz had observed, there were rough edges to Jimmy's game, but his timing and rapid-fire reflexes more than made up for them. His responses were so fast, in fact, that his father once described him as the kind of kid who runs to the door even before the doorbell rings.

In keeping with this natural ability, his mother and grandmother encouraged him to hit the ball early when it came over the net, to keep opponents off-balance. It made the game fast, which was perfect for Jimmy. Rather than wait for the ball to arc back toward the ground after a bounce, he attacked it right after the bounce. It demanded superb timing and split-second adjustment—which were part of Jimmy's arsenal—and lots of practice and coaching, which his family supplied in abundance.

To help him develop his hammerlike hitting, especially on return of service, Mom and Two-Moms took Jimmy to practice on the varnished floor of the St. Louis Armory. "Dances and drills made that floor mean," Jimmy said, "and I had to hit the ball early, challenge every serve, pick it up, and sweep at it before it could spin away."

Without the advantage of size (Jimmy weighed about fifty pounds when he was ten years old), he knew that success depended on speed and technique. Jimmy worked like a demon to make up the difference.

From the age of eight, Jimmy was skillful enough to be entered in major tournaments for boys every year and to make a good showing in competition. He won his first championship in the ten-year-old-and-under group in the Southern Illinois tournament. Usually, though, he would be eliminated from major competition by the quarterfinal round. It wasn't because he couldn't hack it; he simply didn't have the size and weight yet. Most of Jimmy's opponents could lift him up and carry him around the court—he was that small.

Plenty of kids would have given up trying to be athletes if they were as short and skinny as he was, but Jimmy was hooked on tennis and refused even to think of quitting. Others, like his brother Johnny, would have given up because it took so much time and work. Nothing stopped Jimmy.

After graduating from the eighth grade at St. Philip School, in 1966, Jimmy entered Assumption Catholic High in East St. Louis. Naturally he joined the tennis team. The school's athletic director, Dick Ryan, remembered Jimmy as "a charming little guy. But he was so tiny you'd never have thought he could have accomplished what he did."

The boy in Mr. Ryan's memory was five feet tall and weighed around ninety pounds—hardly the ordinary picture of what an athlete looks like. But "ordinary" is not the word to describe Jimmy Connors, and if confidence is the distinguishing mark of a sports hero, then Jimmy had it by the ton.

The summer before his freshman year at Assumption Jimmy had been entered in the Triple A Invitational tournament at Forest Park, Illinois. He did extremely well in the early matches, cutting down every opponent on his way up the elimination-rounds ladder. Then he was faced with a match against the formidable Chuck McKinley. The top seed in the tournament, McKinley was an adult who already had years of experience on the international tennis circuit.

On the day before they met, Jimmy asked his mother, "If I beat McKinley, can I turn pro?"

Gloria Connors smiled at her son's confidence in

himself. "Sure," she said, "pro at thirteen."

And Jimmy answered his own question the next day, when he lost to Chuck McKinley, 6–4, 6–2.

To some observers Jimmy Connors has always seemed like a smart-alecky guy with a huge ego. They may admire his winning tennis, yet that won't change their opinion of his personality. But these people don't understand that the enormous ego was necessary for him to become a star. Either they don't know about Jimmy's childhood, or they choose to ignore the fact that he was so tiny, so thin and unmuscular.

Jimmy's many critics also forget that a huge ego is just another way of saying that he believed in himself even when there was no solid proof that he would amount to something. The outside world looked at and listened to Jimmy Connors, saw and heard an outspoken champion, and wondered why he wasn't more modest. But champion or not, Jimmy remembered when confidence was all he had to go on, when he was Mr. Ryan's "charming little guy." Maybe the superbig, natural athletes can afford to be modest. Others, like the Little Prince of Belleville, need the psych of a big ego.

At Assumption High, in his freshman year, Jimmy was among the best of the tennis players, although he was a head shorter than some of his teammates. He was so good, in fact, that he was chosen to represent the school at the Illinois State High School tournament. There, he battled his way up through the early rounds, only to be eliminated in the quarterfinals. He didn't like losing one bit, but the loss couldn't chip away any of the confidence that was built inside him like a block of granite. Someday, the little freshman was sure, he would beat every one of them.

To make that dream a reality, he never let up on practicing and learning his tennis trade. Every day of Jimmy's life was structured around the court. "Jimmy didn't take Phys. Ed.," Mr. Ryan said. "We had it arranged so his mother and grandmother would pick him up in the last period so he could go to tennis practice."

It might have been fun to horse around in gym with the other guys, but Jimmy's golden goal made that a luxury he couldn't afford.

During his sophomore year at Assumption Jimmy didn't play for the school team. A choice was given him: Play for the school, or play amateur tennis on the junior U.S. Lawn Tennis Association (USLTA) circuit. It wasn't an easy decision to give up the varsity team. Jimmy liked the school spirit behind the team, and he liked the other players. But the competition was better on the amateur schedule, and it was the more direct route to where he wanted to go. After weighing the facts, he quit the school team.

It turned out to be a wise choice. Later that year, the Connors family moved from St. Louis to the town of Belleville. Jimmy would not be attending Assumption in his junior year, and becoming emotionally attached to the team would have made the school change harder.

Belleville, Illinois, was a quiet suburban community of nice houses and pleasant streets. But for Jimmy, a hometown (nice or not) was merely a place to be from. His energy was totally centered on where he was going, not where he was, and only tennis could determine that.

After briefly considering the public high school in Belleville, Jimmy's parents registered him at Althoff Catholic High School. The Connors didn't make a big show of their religion, but they were devout Catholics. The Connors boys attended parochial school from the time they entered kindergarten, and never wavered from their faith. For Jimmy in particular, a system that emphasized hard work and attention to duty was just right. He was never a rebel or a cutup in school. He never tried to be one of the guys, was never subjected to peer pressure to do things he didn't want to do to win the approval of others his age. All Jimmy really cared about was following his personal star, the one that he dreamed would one day shine above the entire world of tennis.

3

Jimmy the Giant Killer

Jimmy had a problem. Sure, his tennis was getting slicker every year as he grew into his teens, but improvement wasn't coming fast enough to satisfy the win-hungry kid. Every year he'd hit the same barrier—size. With his split-second reflexes, excellent return of service, and perfectly placed ground shots, Jimmy would pull himself through the early rounds of the age-group tournaments. Then, coming into the final rounds, he'd have to take on rivals with no more ability but much more physical advantage. It was a handicap that Jimmy simply couldn't overcome.

All along, however, there was no doubt that Jimmy had the stuff to become a champion—if only he'd start growing. His class showed in doubles matches, in which he was tops. Paired with Brian Gottfried, of Fort Lauderdale, Florida, Jimmy won the twelve-and-under-boys' doubles in 1964, and the fourteen-and-under doubles in '66. Having a partner, though, wasn't anywhere near the same as winning by yourself. And doubles victories, while they were written into the record books, just didn't have the glory of singles victories. To be a tennis star—and Jimmy would settle for nothing less—depended on winning those big singles matches. Right now, though, that was impossible without the addition of a few inches in height and the muscle to go with them.

Mrs. Connors knew how her son felt about the sport, and she wondered if the wonderful future he dreamed of would ever be. "Gloria kept worrying," Mr. Connors said, "that Jimmy might be a runt. But I kept telling her there weren't any short people in my family or any short people in her family, so how could he be a runt?"

In 1968 the waiting and worrying began to come to an end. Jimmy had, at last, started to grow taller. And with every additional inch he became more effective on the court—running farther, reaching higher, bringing to bear more power and thrust in his strokes. Of course, he'd need more time for his body to catch up by putting more meat on his lengthening bones. But that weight would come naturally, and the future grew brighter with each additional inch.

He also grew as a tennis player, because 1968 was the year that Jimmy put it all together, hammering his way through the sixteen-and-under competition until he reached the final round of the national championship tournament. Just one more match to win, and Jimmy would be ranked as the best male tennis player of his age in the country. It was a great feeling—and a scary one—to be so close. And it made every sweating, aching hour of practice worth the effort.

Jimmy tried to be calm as he walked onto the court in Kalamazoo, Michigan, for the finals against Alex Mayer, Jr. It wouldn't be easy. Mayer was a rugged foe, a more experienced player than Jimmy, and not the kind to give away any points or fade when the going got tight.

On his side, Jimmy could show he was far from a pushover. He owned that whopper of a backhand, speed, and a self-confidence that knew no limits. And to take advantage of these assets, he had a simple strategy for the upcoming match—jump on everything hit his way, break Mayer's serve, set the pace, wear down and overpower his opponent.

The court action was James Scott Connors at his finest. From the first, he took command of the play, and he stayed in charge all the way. It was a swift, overwhelming victory—6–3, 6–1. The dynamic, hard-hitting young man was now the boys' champion tennis player in the United States. He did he like it? Jimmy's grin as Mayer congratulated him said more than a million words could have. His expression was a picture of pride and pleasure.

Nevertheless, age-group competition in tennis, as in other sports, meant a new start every year. As a competitor reached the cutoff age, he'd move up to the next group and have to deal with a new set of opponents, each one the cream of the crop from the age-group below.

This gave Jimmy something to think about. Since

he turned sixteen on September 2, 1968, he could, if he wanted to, remain in his age-group until his seventeenth birthday. But if he played in the sixteen-and-under class much longer, it might be bad for him. If he didn't move up now, he was sure to be a consistent winner and repeat as "king of the kids." On the other hand, if he did move up right away, to take on the bigger and stronger eighteen-and-unders, he stood a good chance of losing a number of matches.

Weighing the values of winning over easy competition against taking on the challenge of the next level (called juniors), Jimmy had to ask himself: What good would it do to win against younger kids when, on September 2, 1969, he'd have to be ready for the older ones? The more he thought about it, the more his choice became clear—he had to do it the hard way. He'd dive into junior tennis long before the age of seventeen forced him to make the move.

A player with less ego would have made the move just for the valuable experience, even though he wouldn't have any real hope of being a winner. Not Jimmy. He never set foot on a tennis court without intending to come out the conqueror. So what if his opponents were bigger and older and had more savvy? Indoors or outdoors, hard court or soft court, in any kind of condition—Jimmy was ready to play . . . and to win.

Asked at the time why he thought he could do well in junior competition, Jimmy replied, "I have an all-round game—good backhand, good forehand, good serve. And nothing in an opponent has ever bothered me.'' Maybe he should have been scared, but he wasn't.

It was a credit to Jimmy's drive, and his mother's coaching, that he did fairly well in the 1969 season. He reached the outdoor junior semifinals in Kalamazoo, Michigan, and then was defeated by Richard Stockton, 6–4, 4–6, 6–3. Not only was his reaction one of satisfaction, but he actually felt great about his showing. The Connors confidence was as strong as ever. Even though he had lost, Jimmy had taken one set and had made Stockton fight for every point. Just wait till he played Stockton again. . . .

Then Jimmy reached the finals of the junior indoor championships later in the year, only to drop a real battle to Roscoe Tanner, 6–3, 10–8. It was a heart-breaker for Jimmy. He had used everything he had to keep the second set going, determined to wear down his opponent. But Tanner's sizzling serve and strong net game proved to be a little too much, upsetting Jimmy's strategy by keeping him on the defensive.

The time had come for a big decision, a radical change in Jimmy's life. Gloria Connors recognized it before Jimmy did, and she talked to him about it. She had taken him as far as she could. He needed a new coach, someone who could help him develop a volley game and build up his serve. He also needed to be some place where he could play outdoors every day. Living in Belleville and playing in the old armory had been fine until now. At this point Jimmy needed better conditions. However, he had to decide if he wanted success so much that he'd be willing to leave home and live elsewhere for a while.

Jimmy wasn't happy about the idea of leaving his home and his family. He had never been away before except for tournaments, and those lasted only a few days. Besides, his mother had always gone with him. He might have been a big-time tennis player, but underneath he was still a small-town boy. Still, he knew he had come to another crossroads in his young life. He weighed the negative things against the positive things, and again his decision was: Let's do it.

Once the decision was made, the next important concern was finding the right coach and mentor. Gloria Connors pondered it long and hard, determined to not make a hasty decision. It had to be someone who wouldn't disturb her son's natural style of play, someone who would know how to help Jimmy capitalize on his assets and add to his skills. At last, Mrs. Connors traveled out to California to see Francisco Segura, known as Pancho to millions of tennis fans.

Segura, a former touring pro, was regarded as one of the most experienced coaches in the country. His knowledge and skill could work wonders for any young star he took under his wing. The question was: Would he be interested in working with the kid from Illinois? The Connors family had high hopes that he would. "My mom," Jimmy said, "had been on the circuit with Pancho in the old days. And she knew I was more like him than any other of the famous players. So she spoke to him, and he said, 'I'll make the arrangements.'

"Two weeks later," Jimmy continued, "he phoned to say that I would be going into my senior year at Rexford High School in Los Angeles with his son, Spencer, and that he would play with me at the Beverly Hills Tennis Club where he was the pro."

At first, the plan was for Jimmy to board with a family in California. Then, because it seemed a better idea, and with Mr. Connors' agreement, Mrs. Connors decided to go with her son. In California she would rent a small apartment near the tennis club, to create a home away from home. That way Jimmy would have a sense of security to bolster him in his new school and with his new coach. Furthermore, to cover some of the costs of the very expensive move, Mrs. Connors planned to do some tennis teaching in Los Angeles. The whole family agreed that these were the best possible arrangements.

In years to come, some writers would criticize Mrs. Connors (and her mother, Mrs. Thompson, who accompanied her) for moving to the West Coast with Jimmy. They said that she didn't want to let go of her son. But at the time of the move most observers believed that she was doing the right thing.

"Jimmy may be seventeen years old, but in some ways he's a real little kid," a West Coast tennis pro said. "If Gloria had sent him here alone, they would have devoured him. I mean, all the smooth, sophisticated kids at the club and at Rexford. You know, California isn't the Midwest. Things are a century ahead here—teenagers zipping around in flashy cars, rich kids throwing away money like used tissues, drugs, rock . . . the whole scene. No way that Jimmy could have survived without a parent around keeping an eye on him."

A friend of the family in Illinois made another point. "When Gloria talked about Jimmy going to California," she said, "you should have heard the reaction! 'You're shipping him off?' one woman asked. Another one said that only an unnatural parent would do anything like that. Gloria couldn't please everybody—if she stayed home, she'd be a cruel mother; if she went with Jimmy, she'd be a clinging mother. You can't win."

There was never any doubt that Jimmy was happy to have his mother and grandmother in California, even though he had very little time with them. "I'd leave our apartment at seven-thirty every morning," he said, "tell my mom and grandmother, 'Have a nice day,' and I wouldn't be home until it was almost dark. Every day I'd play tennis."

Pancho Segura had arranged for Jimmy to have only morning classes at Rexford High, leaving afternoons free for tennis. If the school had an afternoon activity scheduled and he was supposed to attend, Jimmy would slip out anyway. "Segu or my mother," Jimmy explained, "would simply sign a note the next day so I could play some more tennis."

Jimmy was a bright boy who might have been a good student if he had cared, but he never paid more than the minimum attention to schoolwork. All he wanted was to pass his courses. When he did, he was satisfied. But put him out in the sun, between the baselines, and he'd never give up. Spencer Segura, his best friend, described Jimmy as having an "amazing hunger" to learn tennis.

Pancho Segura was the perfect teacher for Jimmy. Never the most powerful player, the five-foot-seven-inch-tall Segura had become a pro by using the right stroke at the right time, out-thinking his opponents. He was a master of court strategy, and even more important for a coach, he knew just how to explain his winning theories. Every day, after he worked on the court with Jimmy, Segura would sit the boy down and talk tennis, sketching plays on a paper napkin.

"I learned the most right there," Jimmy said. "Segu would talk about the old days and tell stories. He'd go over situations, draw exchanges and positions, and show me what percentage certain shots had of working and when to hit them. It was fascinating."

After working with Jimmy for only a short time, Segura was certain that the kid could go all the way to the top, if he learned to play "smart" tennis. Unlike most other pros, Segu had used a two-handed stroke on backhand shots and didn't consider the technique a sign of weakness. Furthermore, standing five-seven himself, he didn't feel that Jimmy, who had by now almost reached his adult height of five-ten, was too small for the sport. The key to being a champ, Segura insisted, was concentration—and Jimmy had that.

"He's in another world with a racket in his hands," Segura said of his young protégé. "He's capable of concentrating for two hours—and a lot of guys can't come close to that."

Jimmy had something else going for him: his ferocious desire to win. Too often a player with the superior skills can lose a match to an inferior, by "coasting" when he's ahead or by trying to be a "nice guy" on the court. Let up for a moment, go easy on an opponent who's a friend—and you're dead. The only way to be a consistent winner, and Jimmy always knew it, is to be tough and relentless all the way.

Sometimes, when he was a young boy practicing with his mother in Illinois, Jimmy would forget the lesson of toughness, and he'd play soft. And each time he did it, Gloria Connors would wallop the ball at him. "When he was young," she said, "if I had a shot I could hit down his throat, I did. And I'd say, 'See, Jimmy, even your mother will do that to you.' "

It was in keeping with the same lessons Pancho taught—hang in there; never give an inch; save your friendships for off-court hours. This attitude, so similar to what he had been given before, made

Jimmy feel comfortable about taking instruction from Segura.

The relationship of coach and pupil was very fruitful. When Jimmy goofed on a shot or acted silly, Segura came down hard. Fortunately those moments were rare. Jimmy respected the wily old player and behaved well in his presence. In return, Segura had much praise for Jimmy.

"He'll never have a great serve," was the worst Segura said of his eager student. "But it's good . . . adequate." To balance that, Segura went on to say, "Jimmy can adjust according to his opponent. He can play offense and defense. He has all-court control. He moves back and in. He can play at net and baseline. He hits high shots and low shots. He knows how to lob behind the baseline to make you earn the point. Tennis matches are lost when you try to attack and you shouldn't.

"Jimmy has been taught to think," Segura added, "to play the vital points, to serve the first ball in. You know, tennis is a sport where you can win more games but still lose the match." The point was, he made abundantly clear, to win the match. That was what you were there to do.

One of the bits of luck in Jimmy's favor was that he was left-handed, while most of his opponents were right-handed. Normally tennis players are stronger and more accurate on forehand strokes. So, as Jimmy explained, "A right-handed player has a tendency to hit to my forehand [because right-handers think of the left-hand side of the court as the weak, backhand side], and I can hit everything else with my two-handed backhand.''

Everything was fitting into place for Jimmy now. His game grew stronger, and with it his ever-present confidence. He couldn't wait to get out on the court in a tournament and stun the world with what he could do. But shrewd Pancho Segura advised patience, and even further tuning up, before turning his tennis machine loose in tournament play. He didn't want Jimmy to rush out and fall on his face. He knew that self-confidence is a tricky and sometimes frail quality. So he brought in another old pro to apply the finishing touches to his eager and willing pupil.

4

The Master Touch

Jimmy Connors was a cocky young man who was seldom in awe of anybody. But on the day that Richard Gonzales came to the Beverly Hills Tennis Club to rally with him, Jimmy gulped. Gonzales (nicknamed Pancho, like Segura) had been a superstar of tennis before Jimmy was born and was still a formidable opponent. For a novice, playing tennis against Gonzales was like a young basketball player today being told to go one-on-one with Wilt Chamberlain. The veteran star might be retired from active play, he might not have the stamina or speed of his youth, but he could still kill you. Just the thought of the man's past greatness and the suspicion that he might have forgotten more than you'd ever learn could make a kid nervous. And Jimmy Connors certainly was nervous about facing Pancho Gonzales.

To start off, the master would just hit a few with the pupil. Gonzales didn't say much; he didn't try to give advice or change Jimmy's style. He was teaching by example, hitting shots that forced Jimmy to work and think. The youngster might have had all the confidence in the world, but that would not be enough in top-level tennis. There were too many guys up there who could literally overpower him.

Gonzales had developed power tennis to a fine art. The question was: Could he teach it to Connors? He was going to try. The main problem, as Gonzales saw it, was timing. Gloria Connors and Pancho Segura had encouraged Jimmy to attack the ball, to go to it rather than let it come to him. And Jimmy, with his speed and sharp reflexes, had taken well to this style. It worked brilliantly on return of service, Jimmy's favorite weapon. While an opponent was still trying to get into position after serving, Jimmy would smash a return with precise timing. Sometimes the other player couldn't reach the ball in time, and Jimmy would win a point immediately. Other times his opponent would get to the ball but return it so weakly that Jimmy would have a "cripple" to hammer home for the point. Either way, it would be a winner if it worked.

The trouble was that it didn't *always* work. First of all, no shot could go in right every time. Also, it was too predictable, and soon every player who faced Jimmy learned his strategy and knew just what to expect. He might beat them once, maybe even twice, but eventually the good ones would come up with a defense to neutralize Jimmy's "supermove." So he had reached the point at which he had to stock his arsenal with other weapons, and Gonzales was there to guide him. There wasn't a better combat veteran for the job.

"Maybe I can help his game," the two-time U.S. Nationals champ said. "Bring on his potential a little sooner. I do know I have helped him on pace. Jimmy has a tendency to rush himself too much."

Slow down, that was the message Gonzales was sending across the net. Stall for time when you need it; change the pace of the game if it's going against you. . . . Jimmy got the message and steadily began adding some of the master's techniques to his game. Among them was the tactic of bouncing the ball a dozen or more times before serving. Another was stepping off the court for a few seconds to delay an opponent's serve, to break the other player's rhythm and concentration. They were tricks, not pure tennis, but they had an effect on the game. In fact, they could be as effective as a perfectly placed dropshot.

In later years Jimmy's stalling tactics would irritate observers, as well as opponents. They were sure he did these things to be mean and because he didn't like the other players. But it wasn't so. All the little gimmicks that surrounded Jimmy's basic game were taught to him as strategy to strengthen that basic game.

In the same way, Jimmy would one day be bad-mouthed for his single-minded aggressiveness on the court. That was because he never gave the feeling that he was playing a game against a friend and colleague. It was always a battle for supremacy, and anyone holding a racket on the other side of the net was automatically a threat to slow Jimmy's climb to the top of the hill. This, too, was an attitude drilled into Jimmy by his coaches, Segura and Gonzales. Gonzales, particularly, had made it a habit to come on the court fiercely and to maintain a warlike expression throughout tennis matches. It was the same kind of psychology Muhammad Ali used before fights—never say anything nice about the other guy; don't be afraid of being the "bad guy"; don't show fear or uncertainty. Jimmy was instructed to do the same, and he found that it paid off. It might not be the way to become popular, but it kept Jimmy focused on his game—and winning, which was what he wanted more than anything else. He definitely didn't want to be a well-liked loser.

During the winter of 1969–70 Pancho Gonzales began setting up doubles matches with Jimmy as his partner. It was a devastating combination—the old warhorse and the eager kid—and it helped Jimmy a great deal. "Pancho calms me down," he said, "shows me the right strokes, and coaches me on strategy. I know it's a heavy responsibility, playing next to such a great player, but it doesn't bother me anymore."

As Gonzales' partner Jimmy began to catch the attention of the tennis world. There are always plenty of good players on the junior level, but people felt that only a special youngster would ever be invited to share a court with a giant of the game like Pancho

Gonzales. This, perhaps more than anything else, brought Jimmy to public notice in the spring and summer of 1970.

Competitively, Jimmy was having a good year. He won the Junior National Hardcourt Championship and the Junior National Clay Court Championship. He was named a member of the junior Davis Cup team, he was a semifinalist in the Junior Outdoor Nationals, and he was doing well against players on the adult circuit. That was most important of all, because it was the test of whether he'd survive in the arena where the sport's real craftsmen held forth. So, when he upset Roy Emerson and Ray Moore in the Pacific Southwest tournament, Jim McManus in the Thunderbird, and even reached the finals of the Southern California Men's tournament—where he lost to none other than Pancho Gonzales—everyone agreed this was a "comer" well worth watching.

September, 1970, saw Jimmy in his first match at the very top level of the international circuit. It was at Forest Hills, in New York. "I had called the West Side Tennis Club," Jimmy said, "to inquire about entering. When I asked about the doubles, they told me Gonzales already had entered us as a team. It was a funny feeling."

Walking onto the practice courts before the tournament was even "funnier." There, waiting, were reporters from all the major newspapers around the world—and they immediately began asking questions of him. Jimmy would turn eighteen during the

1970 U.S. Nationals at Forest Hills, but at the moment he didn't feel very grown-up. It wasn't easy fielding the questions, knowing the right thing to say, the right way to behave. And, on all sides of him, there were dozens of famous players practicing and being interviewed, greeting people they knew, forming off-court groups. Jimmy, the loner, stayed a bit apart from the others. Maybe he would have liked being welcomed and made to feel one of them, but he wasn't. Nobody set out to cut Jimmy cold, keep him "in his place." They simply didn't know the newcomer, so they paid no attention to him. And he, without meaning to, gave the impression that he wanted nothing to do with them.

Every novice has encountered the situation Jimmy went through at his first U.S. Nationals. And every one of them has had to work out a way of dealing with it. Jimmy's way was to erect a wall and to act as if he didn't care. He hadn't learned, when he was younger, how to be a friend, and he didn't know what to do now. But he really felt no hostility to anyone in tennis—he hadn't been around long enough to have enemies any more than friends.

Those people who were nice to Jimmy when he was a newcomer discovered a shy young man behind the defensive barrier he showed to the world. They also discovered a nice guy with a good sense of humor and a guy who was completely loyal to his few friends. After Jimmy became the world's most famous tennis player, by which time his lone-wolf ways had made him many enemies, he always spoke well of Rumanian Ilie Nastase. "Nasty was different," Jimmy said, "from the other guys when I met him. He was a top star, and he hardly spoke any English, and he took an interest in me, a kid." Jimmy's tone made it clear that he wished the others would have done the same.

In the long run, the experiences Jimmy had off the court at his first Forest Hills tournament would matter more than how he played that year. But at the time it was tennis that was uppermost in his mind. He did play, singles and doubles, and make his name known. In singles play, he wasn't fortunate in the player he drew and was eliminated in an early round. In doubles, however, he and Pancho Gonzales proved to be a strong combination. The forty-two-year-old man and the eighteen-year-old boy mowed down opponents to reach the quarterfinals, ousting such impressive pairs as Tom Okker and Marty Riessen and Terry Addison and Bob Carmichael.

The Gonzales-Connors duo showed a definite style in their first two matches, attaining peaks of near perfection whenever the score was close. Both matches went into tie-breaker sets, and both were nip-and-tuck contests throughout. In the Addison-Carmichael vs. Gonzales-Connors meeting Addison had the serve at match point. Win this one and wrap it up, Carmichael told himself. He had the choice of hitting to the cunning old master or the kid.

Gonzales looked weary, as if his age had finally

overtaken his skills. But, as close as anyone of his time could come to it, he was Mr. Tennis. Even a timeworn tiger could have a fatal bite left in him. Connors, on the other hand, looked as fresh as when he started. Under the hot sun, on that muggy day, he seemed to have scarcely perspired. Still, he was inexperienced, and he had to be nervous. There was a fair chance he'd make a mistake, overplay the ball, choke on the big one.

Addison made his choice, threw the ball into the air, and ripped his serve at Jimmy. Jimmy's answer to the challenge came back in a blur, a ground stroke like a Nolan Ryan fastball and right on the money. It skipped by the frantic lunge of Carmichael for the point that nailed the match for Jimmy and Pancho.

"Jimmy won it," a grinning Gonzales announced proudly after he and his partner had shaken hands with the losing pair. He was obviously pleased that he could pick 'em as well as he could play 'em.

As the reporters crowded around, interviewing the dynamite duo, Gonzales smoothly did most of the talking. When he was asked how they had overcome the generation gap that separated them, the old pro laughed. "I feel I'm the same age as Jimmy," he said in mock seriousness. "I've just been there longer." Jimmy nodded and smiled.

What would they do, a newsman asked, if they won the doubles championship? Gonzales, as a professional, could accept the money prize; Connors, an amateur, was not allowed to. Pancho threw the question right back at the press. "Do I get to keep the whole purse for our team—or half?" he asked. "Didn't Jimmy contribute to my monetary gain? Will that affect his amateur standing? Should he even be allowed to play in a tournament with a professional?"

The questions didn't really matter. In the quarterfinals Connors and Gonzales lost to Patricio Cornejo and Jaime Fillol. There was no prize money to worry about anyway. What did matter, though, was that Jimmy Connors had faced the test of playing against the "big guys" and had shown he belonged on the same court with them.

5

Something Money Can't Buy

Jimmy was forever ready to learn, but what he wanted to learn wasn't taught in a classroom. So, when he enrolled at UCLA in the fall of 1970, the odds were against his staying there long enough to earn a degree. It was far more likely that he would hang around long enough to win the National Collegiate Athletic Association (NCAA) championship and leave school. That title was the "degree" he was after.

Unlike football and basketball, in which school titles carry considerable prestige, high school and college tennis wins are pretty unimportant. The significant junior tournaments are all run by the USLTA (United States Lawn Tennis Association), and some fine competitors never even bother with their school teams. The NCAA crown is the only exception to the rule. Dennis Ralston, Arthur Ashe, Charles Pasarell, Bob Lutz, and Stan Smith had snared the singles title in NCAA competition; now Jimmy Connors wanted to tack his name onto that impressive list.

Gloria Connors and her mother had gone home to

Belleville, Illinois. Jimmy was to live with the other members of the UCLA tennis team under Coach Bassett. Then, as James Connors, Sr., said, "Jimmy got kind of lonesome, so my wife and mother-in-law packed up and went out there again." The whole college scene didn't interest Jimmy, and he preferred the security of a real home to a dormitory. He felt different from the others, and he acted on his feelings.

Jimmy's life at UCLA, though it wasn't given over to much studying, wasn't round-the-clock tennis, either. He spent evenings with his best buddy, Spencer Segura, at many of the local "in" spots, drinking sodas and looking at the girls. Jimmy dated occasionally, but very casually. Aside from his family and the Seguras, he preferred being by himself.

Devoting so much of his days to one thing— tennis—had kept Jimmy too busy to learn how to be smooth or hip. Now he wanted to shed what he referred to as "my cornfield look." He started taking an interest in clothes, buying velvet suits and fancy shoes. He listened to the fast patter that his peers admired and tried to imitate it. He paid attention to cars, picking up on which ones were considered "in." He knew the latest gossip repeated around campus by guys who referred to famous Hollywood people by first names only. In short, Jimmy applied a lot of energy to becoming "slick."

At the same time he had the feeling that the whole

thing was phony. Underneath the glittery surface and glib talk, the idols of Southern California were empty people who never accomplished anything worthwhile. So, even though a part of Jimmy was whispering to him to be like them, a more mature voice inside told him that dedication to a goal had more meaning and value. Jimmy decided to be himself.

After he became a successful pro and college life was far in the past, Jimmy looked back on those early days in California. "I never had any heroes. All the money and the celebs didn't mean anything to me," he said. "I just wanted to play tennis.

"Anyway," he went on, "the movie stars were coming out there to see *me*, to play tennis with *me*. I must have been somebody myself. Here's Dino Martin and rich kids like that hanging around. They get new Ferraris every year, but they aren't responsible people. Never show up on time, forget their friends. Dino wanted to bet me always. He said I had no class, that I'd never get ranked or have my picture on magazine covers. See, he had a famous father and several tons of dough and time on his hands and all the broads. Yet all he wanted to do was to play good tennis. He wanted what I had. So he bet. And if we had kept on playing for money, he probably would have owed me his life."

Once he realized that what he had was something his richer friends could never buy, Jimmy gave up worrying about anything but tennis. He would show them something that *no* amount of cash could buy—that he'd be the best tennis player in the game, ranked right up there with the finest ever.

He was itching to get on with it. First, he had to capture the NCAA crown. Others believed that Jimmy would do well, but that the title would go to some junior or senior on the UCLA team. Let them think what they wanted to. As far as Jimmy was concerned, he wanted it *now*. He worked toward this end through the 1970–71 season, leading his college team in spirit and in wins. He also competed on the indoor USLTA circuit, sharpening his stroke and rolling up an impressive series of victories. Ranked number one in junior tennis, Jimmy was also listed as number fourteen on the adult level.

The UCLA squad traveled to South Bend, Indiana, in the middle of June, 1971, for the NCAAs. Jimmy didn't have the slightest doubt that he was the one the others would have to beat to take the title. In his mind there were no teammates, no friends. Everyone was an enemy to be defeated. He stayed away from everyone, psyching up.

There was no stopping him as Jimmy knocked off one opponent after another. Then on June 19, came the finals—his big moment. The day before, Jimmy had beaten his teammate, Haroon Rahim, in his semifinal match. That had run the string to seven wins in a row, seven satisfying battles.

Roscoe Tanner, of Stanford University, was Jimmy's opponent. He had run up a record equal to Jimmy's to reach the finals. And Tanner had one other thing going for him. In his semifinal match he had swamped Jeff Borowiak, of UCLA, the defending champion of the NCAA. Borowiak had beaten Tanner in the 1970 finals, and Tanner had taken his revenge. Now he, like Jimmy, had a special reason to take the championship match.

The two college stars walked out onto the court, measured each other coolly, and got set for play. It had to be all-out action, nothing cute or fancy, because both relied heavily on power games. Also, both were left-handers, so neither would have the advantage of a forehand in a normally backhand court. But there was one noticeable advantage— Tanner was big, much bigger than the UCLA freshman.

Everything worked exactly right for Jimmy in the opening set. The concentration that had brought him this far was holding firm. Like a horse wearing blinders, he blocked out the off-court distractions. A smashing serve from Tanner, and Jimmy was right there, booming the ball back as if he hated it. Then his serve—hard, sharp, putting Tanner off-balance. The set went to Jimmy, 6–3. Everything was going right on schedule.

At least two sets to go, and Tanner ordered himself not to let the kid jump into the lead again. Tanner bore down and, with his superior strength and size, overpowered Jimmy, forcing mistakes and leaping on easy returns with murderous blows.

First game to Tanner. The crowd's reaction

showed that just about every spectator expected the upperclassman to squash the freshman. And they seemed to be right, as Connors lost service once in the second set and failed to break Tanner's. He seemed to have lost his touch and was rushing, trying desperately to capture the rhythm of play and turn the tide back his way. But every time he appeared to be getting there Tanner pulled ahead again, going on to take the second set, 6–4.

They were dead even, one set apiece. Jimmy took a deep breath, walking around in tight circles. His expression seemed to be saying, This is the big one—lose it and it might be too late.

"You could almost see Jimbo change from a loser to a winner after Roscoe took that set," said a tennis writer present that day. "It was like he had a tape recorder in his head, and he had just switched it on to hear Segura and Gonzales giving him advice. You could see that smile he gets, kind of wise and mean, and Roscoe looked as if he'd jump out of his skin. And Jimmy's serves were terrific—like Gonzales was guiding his hand.

"Nobody could have gone up against him playing like that. When Jimmy took the third set, six-four, he was sailing away with it. Tanner had no chance, although he did fight back doggedly. It's to Roscoe's credit that the fourth set went six-four against him rather than six-zero.

"If you want to get some idea of the match, just check the stats. Tanner broke Connors' service just once in nineteen games. Connors broke Tanner's three times. Tanner double-faulted seven times; Jimmy only four. Jimbo was a living wonder out there. It was like that Babe Ruth story—pointing to the stands and hitting right to the spot. That's the way Jimmy placed his shots. And those serves! I swear, I never saw anything like it for precision."

Jimmy had wanted to show them that he was second to no one, and he had. Jimmy Connors—the first freshman ever to win the NCAA singles championship. It didn't feel good—it felt great!

Jimmy went on the summer circuit with a new billing: James Connors, Jr., NCAA champion. He was also being called "one of the best young prospects" in the game of tennis. People would point him out, study his games carefully, compare him with Stan Smith, Arthur Ashe, and the other current sensations. Wherever Jimmy went, he was in the spotlight, and it was very exciting.

"It makes me feel two ways," Jimmy said. "It makes me feel great to think that what I've done in tennis has made people think of me this way. But it also brings more pressure as I go on. It's the old story. When suddenly you've done well, you're always expected to win."

This was the moment of truth. Lots of young phenoms, in every sport, blaze onto the scene briefly. Then, under the pressure of publicity, they crack and fade from sight. An unknown can lose and never be blamed for it. A titleholder has to keep winning, or the critics say he's finished. It wasn't fair to Jimmy, or to any kid, to have to deal with this kind of pressure. But nobody ever said that life was fair.

Jimmy didn't impress the win-hungry public too much in the summer of 1971. He was playing well, but not drubbing everyone in sight. For Jimmy, however, the summer tour was a success because he was improving. Trained on indoor wooden and outdoor hard-surface courts, he had to learn to adapt his style to the grass and clay surfaces. It was also the time to perfect those serve and volley techniques he had been taught by Gonzales and Segura. In the day-to-day play of the tour, Jimmy was putting together what would be his game in the sensational years to come.

It soon became evident that Jimmy's basic style would have to be closer to Segura's than to Gonzales'. The youngster would never be big enough to rely on a power serve. His foundation for greatness was speed and reflexes, not muscle and size. So he decided to stick to concentrating on his strongest natural talents—precise placement of service returns, burning ground strokes, and aggressive counterpunching.

After a Forest Hills tournament appearance at which he was eliminated in the second round, Jimmy went back to UCLA for his sophomore year. But college was now even less interesting than it had been. After all, he'd gone there originally only to win the NCAAs, and he'd done that. At this point he felt he was spinning his wheels when he wanted to race out and conquer new worlds. And at nineteen he was legally old enough (under the old USLTA rules) to turn pro.

His desires were obvious to those who knew him, but his coach and mother weren't certain that it was the right moment to make the leap into the big time. They were aware, as Jimmy wasn't, that playing one summer wasn't the same as playing pro on a full-time schedule. They had learned, from their own experience, that it could become a grind; that beginners usually went into a slump, and it sometimes finished them; that it was financially wiser to turn pro after coming off a string of wins.

But young Jimmy was straining at the leash. Schoolwork and college competition weren't enough to satisfy his hunger. In his mind were pictures of fame and all that money out there, just waiting to be scooped up by a fast, tireless slugger. It was annoying for him to do well in a tournament, add up the amounts of prize money he would have earned if he'd been a pro, then be forced to accept nothing more than a trophy. And what made it even harder to take was knowing that the Connors family was not rich. Both parents worked, and Jimmy's grandfather sent some of his Social Security money to his grandson every month.

Jimmy didn't want to be a financial burden to his family anymore. They never complained about the cost of his tennis, but he knew that life would be easier if they didn't have to support him. And his gratitude for what they had done for him made him want to shoulder some of the load. So, when the 1971–72 winter indoor tennis season approached, Jimmy became increasingly certain that leaving college to turn pro was the right thing to do.

It was just when the season began, in January, 1972, that Jimmy made the jump. He was in Baltimore, Maryland, playing in a tournament. Everything was going beautifully, and he found himself in the finals against Ilie Nastase. The Rumanian beat him, and Jimmy accepted his second-place trophy. But just getting to the finals against a top player like Nastase clinched Jimmy's resolve to make the move.

"It started me thinking," Jimmy said. "I had to turn down something like eighteen hundred dollars prize money because I was an amateur." To his way of thinking, no trophy was worth that kind of cash.

His mind made up, Jimmy phoned his mother. "I'm going for the money," he told her. "I'm turning pro."

Gloria Connors didn't argue with her son. He wasn't a kid anymore; he was a man who had to make his own decisions.

The next week, in Jacksonville, Florida, Jimmy competed for money. "It was my first tournament as a pro," he remembered happily, "and I won it. I got three thousand dollars for that. Not bad for four days."

He took first prize in his second tournament, at

Roanoke, Virginia. And if he needed any proof that he had made the right choice, this was it. Then he played in Omaha, New York, and Los Angeles, reaching the semifinals in each of the competitions. Jimmy was moving up fast. In fact, he was the hottest player on the circuit, winning five tournaments and finishing high—and in the money—in every other one he entered.

The cash was pouring in so fast Jimmy realized he needed a manager to handle his finances. His choice was Bill Riordan, an independent tour promoter. Riordan, a shrewd businessman, had once been the director of the USLTA indoor circuit and was wise in the ways of tennis. As professional tennis began to capture the interest and money of the sports-viewing public, Riordan started to organize a tour of "his" players. It would be an independent group, not tied to the larger World Championship Tennis (WCT) tour. The WCT had signed most of the big tennis pros and would have liked to add the name of Connors to their list. Riordan advised Jimmy that this wasn't too good an idea for him.

"I told Jimmy," Riordan said, "if you want to be number two in one of the WCT groups, you'll be a nonentity. But if you want to be the best-known player in the world, come with me." Jimmy took Riordan's advice and offer.

Everything was happening so fast. When 1972 had begun, Jimmy was a college student and an amateur. By March he was a successful touring pro and a member of the U.S. Davis Cup team. W. Harcourt Woods, chairman of the Davis Cup Committee, made the announcement that the American squad would consist of Stan Smith, Erik Van Dillen, Tom Gorman, and Jimmy Connors. Jimmy bubbled when he heard the news. "I guess I always dreamed about playing for the Davis Cup," he said.

The team traveled to Jamaica, West Indies, for the first round of matches. Jimmy, the eager new boy, desperately wanted to play for his country's team. But Dennis Ralston, the captain, decided to put his more experienced players into the key singles matches. Jimmy, in bitter disappointment, rode the bench. It struck him as terribly unfair. Maybe the other guys had played longer, but his recent indoor record should have carried some weight.

There was also a rumor that Jimmy was being passed over because of his association with Riordan. All the others on the Davis Cup team, including Ralston, were connected with Donald Dell and the WCT. Maybe it was pure tennis strategy rather than political infighting, but too many people suggested that Jimmy was deliberately being put on ice. If so, it was a cruel way to get back at Riordan. Jimmy couldn't help hearing about these suspicions, but he was too shy to confront the others to get a straight answer.

While Jimmy was in the West Indies, a sad message reached him. His beloved grandmother, Bertha Thompson, had died suddenly in Los

Angeles. The news crushed Jimmy. Two-Moms had been so much more than a grandma, and now he'd never see her again. She'd done so much to help him get this far. It was painful to realize that she hadn't lived to see him reach the very top because he knew how much pride and pleasure she had taken out of his continued success.

Emotionally spent, Jimmy left the team and flew home. There were a number of people who didn't know what had happened, and they were sure to say that he was running away because he had been passed over for play. Let them think what they want; Jimmy didn't stop to explain or to justify himself to them. Right now, his mother needed him, and going to her was the only thing to do.

6

More Firsts for Jimmy

On the courts Jimmy was blazing away. In his first three months as a pro he earned $35,000 in prize money, and observers estimated that he would probably finish the year over the $100,000 mark. Along with the financial reasons for his happiness, he had another cause for excitement: his upcoming trip to Europe, his first, to take part in the most important of all international tennis tournaments—Wimbledon.

But off the courts Jimmy was feeling down. The death of his grandmother had hit him hard. He also found being on the tennis tour a lonely experience. A loner by nature, Jimmy was more isolated than ever. It was partly the result of his having chosen Riordan's tour instead of the WCT, a move many other players resented. It was also partly caused by the hostility shown by established stars, who traditionally react that way toward a youngster who threatens to dethrone them. Most of all, however, it was Jimmy's own doing. He simply did not care to go through the social behavior needed to make friends. Still, it wasn't pleasant when the other men went out to dinner together and didn't invite him along. A solitary hotel room in a strange city and eating alone in a restaurant filled with strangers made for a pretty bleak existence. When they could, Mrs. Connors, Pancho Segura, and Bill Riordan tried to cheer Jimmy, but they couldn't really meet his needs. They were of the older generation, and Jimmy wanted someone of his own age to kid around with.

When he arrived in London, in June, 1972, Jimmy was determined to concentrate on tennis and nothing else. There were a few practice days, to be followed by the Queen's Cup tournament, and, finally, Wimbledon. Both tournaments would be staged on grass courts, and Jimmy needed every bit of practice he could squeeze in. Although grass wasn't a totally unfamiliar surface to him—the courts at the West Side Tennis Club in Forest Hills were grass—Jimmy didn't have the experience on them that the older pros did.

It took work and thinking. Grass courts were tricky, making the ball do crazy things. One day they might be slippery from the rain, and a player would slide like an ice skater who had lost his balance. Another day they might churn up into mud under a player's pounding feet or, on yet another day, be dry and dusty after the sun had baked the surface. And the ball was affected by the conditions. After one bounce it might become heavy with moisture, brown and sticky with mud, mottled with grass stains. Or it might fly off the surface like a hard-rubber ball off concrete. And English courts, the players agreed, were the toughest to play because of the weather. The surfaces were almost always damp and often sodden.

The weather alone was something Jimmy had to adjust to. Coming from California, outdoor tennis meant clear, sunny days to him. But in England, if tennis players waited for a stretch of sunshine, they'd hardly ever get to play. One of the jokes there was: Anything short of a total rainstorm was considered playing weather, even for the biggest tournaments. Jimmy had to be prepared for the discomfort; that was why he set his mind to spend every possible minute on the courts, practicing.

It was during one such practice session before the Queen's Cup that something new, something different was introduced into Jimmy's life. There, on another court, was a pretty, blonde American girl. Jimmy had seen her around at tournaments and had spoken to her briefly two years before. Then she'd been a kid he'd hardly noticed. Now, at seventeen and a half, Chris Evert looked very attractive to him. Casually Jimmy asked her if she'd have a soda with him, and Chris said, "Okay."

It turned into a pleasant hour of conversation between two teenagers. They talked about people they knew, about tennis and the two-handed backhand which they both used, and about the tournaments in which they were entered. Two American kids on their first trip abroad, Chris and Jimmy had a lot in common. Their fathers had gone to college together; they both were Catholic; they enjoyed the same music and TV programs; they had the same goal—to be the greatest tennis player on earth.

There was something else they had in common, though Jimmy and Chris probably didn't realize it at the time. Both were loners, not part of the social life on the tennis circuit. They were also younger than most of the other players and in need of friends their own age. Traveling all the time, they had little chance to date and relax, the way kids their age normally do.

After their informal date, Jimmy had to give up any thought of relaxing. There was a tournament to play. And how he played! Unveiling a power that surprised those who knew him and completely overwhelming those who had never played him, the boy from Belleville made it to the finals at the Queen's Cup. In the title match he was going to take on John Paish of England. Paish, a twenty-four-year-old, had upset Stan Smith in the quarterfinals and beaten Pancho Gonzales in the semifinals. He was a local favorite, he knew the courts and conditions as only a native can, and he was coming off two big wins.

After watching Chris Evert win the women's singles early on that June 24, Jimmy strode out to the court to play his match. He may have been the underdog, but from the first serve of the first game of the first set the outcome was clear. He was trouncing Paish. The Englishman couldn't figure out how to combat this American tornado. Jimmy's serves were perfect—deep and sure and strategically placed. On top of that, his left-handed delivery kept throwing Paish off stride.

The English crowd was pulling for their guy, but it made no difference. The Yank looked as if he had been touched by magic, and he won the finals in straight sets. The match over, the opponents shook hands at the net. Then Jimmy stood rooted to the spot, grinning like a boy at a surprise birthday party. He gazed toward the stands where his mother sat, applauding. She smiled at him. He waved to her, then to the crowd. His first international tournament, and he was the champion. Wow!

The winner walked off the court, looking for Chris Evert. Finding her in the players' area, he said, "Would you like to wait for me? I'd like to have dinner with you." Chris agreed, and Jimmy went off to take what he called his "normal fifty-minute shower" and to dress for the date. Then the two young champions went off together.

"I knew something was up," Bill Riordan recalled of that evening, "when both Colette Evert and Gloria Connors called me at three in the morning to find out where their kids were."

Where they were, and would be every night for the next two weeks, was out dining and dancing. And Jimmy was as happy as he'd ever been before. The gloom he'd felt when Two-Moms died, the loneliness of the tour, everything else that had made him unhappy—all of it was more bearable because he had

Chrissie to talk to, be with, and share his thoughts and feelings in a way no adult ever could.

She was very good for Jimmy. Because she, too, was a tennis star, Jimmy never had to wonder if she liked him for himself or for his fame. (In fact, at that time, Chris Evert was much more famous than Jimmy Connors.) And in her quiet, sensible way, Chris was a wonderful influence on him. Her calm manner was relaxing; her appreciation of his humor was pleasing and good for his ego. In many ways, they were opposites in personality and had a lot to give each other.

The only jarring note was struck when the press found out about the Jimmy-Chrissie twosome and began to trail them around London. It was embarrassing for them, constantly being photographed and asked if they were in love, engaged, ready to elope. Jimmy tried to keep from blowing up at reporters who had no respect for privacy. They were always ragging him, in print, about his lack of dignity. Where was *their* dignity? Jimmy wanted to know. He refused to talk about his new relationship. Whether or not anyone liked it, this was how it was going to be—his private life was going to remain separate from his public life. The subject was closed.

Fortunately, before that kind of pressure could grow any more intense, the Wimbledon tournament began, and the sportswriters went back to writing sports.

Jimmy's first-round match was against Bob

Hewitt, a formidable South African star. Hewitt, ranked seventh in the world, looked like a sure thing against the kid from the States. Even though Jimmy was the Queen's Cup champ, he was expected to lose without a struggle, as newcomers usually do, and go home. Beyond that predicted result, nothing much was thought about the contest. On the day it was scheduled, 23,000 tennis-wise fans sat in the hazy English sunshine and watched number one seed Stan Smith win his first-round match. That one had been billed as the day's highlight.

Connors and Hewitt emerged from the players' area. Jimmy was unsmiling and tense. This was Centre Court at Wimbledon, the sacred temple of tennis. It was an awesome moment for a green young player. He had to remain cool, not pay any attention to the crowd's noise. Gloria Connors was seated in the stands, rosary beads clutched in her hands. She had done all she could in helping him get this far. Now it was up to Jimmy.

The first set began in a blur, like a film running at twice normal speed. Before Hewitt could settle into his game, the score had shot to 3–0 in favor of Connors. The fans, as taken by surprise as the South African, started to stir. This was the kind of tennis they expected from proved winners, not from upstart kids. Certain things would change; the fans settled back to watch in silence.

Hewitt tried to struggle back. Jimmy was treating the tennis ball like a grenade to be disposed of quickly. And Hewitt did the best he could as the action became all serve and volley, a slam-bang contest of speed and power, with tactical rallies something for two other players.

Like a mad dervish, Jimmy ran here and there, pouncing on the ball, pounding it at Hewitt in a steady stream of bullets. The kid's Prince Valiant hair whipped around his head as he wheeled and whirled, lunged and jumped. And the first set was Connors', 6–3.

The second set wouldn't go as quickly. It couldn't. Hewitt, stung by the first set, was over his surprise. And Jimmy knew that the South African, like a wounded bull, would now be very dangerous. He also knew that the temptation to ease up could be working inside him, that being ahead could lull him into a sense of false security. And even as these thoughts were flooding through his head, Jimmy told himself that this wasn't the time to think, think, think. He had to zero in on *now*, to wipe his mind clean of everything but the upcoming point.

But it wasn't that easy. The experienced Hewitt began gaining control. The score went to 4–3, against Connors. Two more games for Hewitt, and the advantage Jimmy had gained would be gone. He cautioned himself to change the pace, to use strategy in place of pure power.

The crowd mumbled impatiently as Jimmy delayed his serve. He could feel them willing him to get on with it. But he had to do it this way. His serve was weakening, and although Hewitt hadn't broken it yet, it might fail any time now.

Jimmy blew into his left hand as he squinted through the hazy glare. Then, very deliberately, he bounced the ball. Once, twice . . . again and again. Hewitt set for the serve . . . relaxed . . . set again.

A flabby serve arched over the net, and Hewitt slapped it back easily. But even before the South African had hit it, Jimmy had moved to the right place. Like a mind reader, he *knew* where to be, and he was there as the ball came spinning into his backhand. That was it, his money shot, and he cashed in on it. With all the force in his body, Jimmy sent a two-hander blasting deep into Hewitt's backhand court. It landed, like a guided missile, just inside the baseline. The score was tied, 4–4.

The lead changed hands, with both players putting everything they had into each point. At last, with the score at 7–6 in his favor, Jimmy needed one game to take the set. Hewitt needed just one point to tie it up again. Connors served, Hewitt sent it back, and Jimmy whipped his racket around to put the point away. But he flubbed it, swinging off-balance and sending his smashing return out. The score was knotted at 7–7.

Hewitt's serve. Jimmy bent low, rocking back and forth, continually moving. It was unnerving, this snakelike motion as he set for his opponent's serve. Hewitt turned it loose, and as the ball zipped over the net, Jimmy's muscular legs drove his body forward.

Now the snake was striking, and those well-conditioned legs made it a deadly move. Hewitt might have the edge of experience, but Connors had the answer in his superconditioning. He went from a crouch to a spring, a dash, a leap . . . endless, tireless motion guaranteed to wear down the best opponent.

At game point Jimmy hammered a backhand ground stroke diagonally across court into a hole in Hewitt's defense. Hewitt reversed direction, trying to move back and to the side. But he was too late: 8–7, Connors.

Jimmy had snapped Hewitt's service for the first time in the set—revenge for the game before. And he was on the attack. Game point again, and Jimmy placed his serve with pinpoint precision. Instantly he moved to where he knew the return had to come. Hewitt hit the ball and moved near the baseline, anticipating Jimmy's bread-and-butter shot, the withering ground stroke.

At this moment Jimmy proved that those hours of strategy plotting with Pancho Segura hadn't been wasted. As baseball Hall of Famer Willie Keeler once said, the trick was to hit 'em where they ain't. Jimmy sped toward the net, reached up, and rocketed a volley into enemy territory. It landed just inside the sideline, a few yards in front of Hewitt. A few yards that were as good as a million miles. The shot locked up the second set for Jimmy, 9–7.

As the third set got under way, Hewitt fought to stay even. Connors served the first game and took it.

Then Hewitt held his serve: 1–1. Connors made good on his: 2–1, Connors. Hewitt evened it at 2–2. Connors went back up, 3–2, then kept up the pressure on Hewitt's serve, going ahead, 4–2.

All at once, as if by signal, the tension of the match seemed to drain away. People in the arena got up to stretch or turned to talk to each other. Just a cleanup job left for Jimmy, they seemed to be saying, for Hewitt didn't look as if he had much fight left in him. He was waiting for the serve, weary-eyed, sweating, and breathing heavily.

It should have served as a signal for Jimmy to come in for the kill. But instead, he let up and lost the next game. It wasn't that Hewitt outhit him, rather that Jimmy double-faulted and lost his serve. The score was now 4–3, Connors, and Hewitt set to serve. The plucky South African saw that this might be his last chance to get back in the match. If he could just take advantage of Connors' mistake. . . .

It was Jimmy who had opened the door a crack, and it was Jimmy who slammed it shut just as quickly. "My mind started to wander," he remarked later, referring to his double fault, "but then I concentrated on concentrating." And blocking out everything on earth but his opponent and the ball, Jimmy surged on to capture the third set, 7–5.

As he saw the match point hit the ground decisively beyond Hewitt's straining reach, Jimmy's arms shot into the air, and his face split into a grin. The audience stood and applauded. These were discriminating

A study in concentration, Jimmy goes after his opponent's shot.

Getting pointers from Pancho Segura

Up in the air to deliver a smashing forehand shot

Bending low for a return

Teamed up with Ilie Nastase in a doubles match

Jimmy demonstrates all the strength of a major league hitter with his powerful two-fisted backhand shot.

tennis fans, who had seen the finest players perform over the years, and they were cheering for the newcomer. He'd put on a two-hour demonstration of scintillating tennis and they were impressed. They had seen it, and the next day's sports pages repeated it: Jimmy Connors, the boy who upset Bob Hewitt, was somebody to watch.

It appeared as if Jimmy's magic spell would never be broken, as he battered his way up to the quarterfinal round. Then, on July 4, 1972, it came to a sudden end as Ilie Nastase, the fiery-tempered Rumanian, beat him in straight sets. The match had been greatly anticipated because the styles of both players were so interesting and so similar.

The wily Nastase set the tempo, breaking Connors' serve and rapidly taking command of the first set, 4–1. But Connors was full of fight and brought the score to 4–4 with his low, searing two-handers that bull's-eyed into the corners.

Nastase snapped Connors' serve again, going up, 5–4. Jimmy went into his crouch—he wasn't through yet. Nastase served, and Jimmy's racket boomed the ball back at him. Point to Connors. Again . . . and again. Now it was 0–40, Connors, and he needed one more point for the game. But Nastase dug down for another trick that Jimmy wasn't ready for. With an ease that looked impossible, he floated the ball over and past Connors, who stood nailed to the ground as if he'd been hypnotized. Nastase leaped on the psychological edge he had established and kept coming, bringing the score to deuce and then conjuring away the set, 6–4. He had outmagicked Jimmy Connors. The second set proceeded like an instant replay of the first. The score went to 4–4; then Nastase claimed it, 6–4.

In the third set it was obvious that Nastase had got the better of Jimmy, and the Rumanian took it, 6–1. Wimbledon, 1972, was over for the kid from Belleville. He wished it had gone differently, but he was pleased with his overall performance and fair about his opponent. "I played as well as I ever have," Jimmy said, "but when a guy plays like that, there is nothing much I could do. If he hadn't been as alert and quick, a lot of those balls would have boomed right by him."

What Jimmy didn't say, but might have thought, was that next time would be his turn. He was young and going to get even better. Just wait and see.

7

Jimmy and Chris and the Sophomore Slump

There are two kinds of fame in sports. The first comes when an athlete is recognized by fans and other athletes. That was Jimmy Connors' position before he beat Bob Hewitt at Wimbledon. The second kind of fame comes when the general public, including those who don't follow sports, know who you are. Such athletes as Joe DiMaggio, Muhammad Ali and Billie Jean King fall into this category. Jimmy Connors joined them when he came home from Wimbledon.

Suddenly his world became a very public place. When Jimmy was entered in a tournament, his name was the headliner, the big attraction. Players were asked their opinions of him for publication, and Jimmy was expected to make statements about others. Reporters followed him; autograph hunters dogged his heels; promoters were after him to play. The vise of fame had clamped tightly around him.

It was a hectic and successful tennis season. Jimmy brought up his win total to seventy-five tournaments, and his cash total for the year went over the $90,000 mark. At Forest Hills he was edged out in the first round by Tom Gorman but still was ranked number three in the country. Had Jimmy done better at the Nationals, he would have been moved up to the number two spot. Even so, though he wanted more than anything to be the best, Jimmy was far from disappointed by his first professional tour.

After Forest Hills, Jimmy entered a new phase of his life. Home had always been made for him by a parent. Now he was on his own, and he decided to move to Fort Lauderdale, Florida, to be near his girlfriend. He took a small apartment, without a phone, near the Evert house. His days were spent in practice and in relaxation before the winter indoor tour, and his evenings were spent with Chris.

Except for the warm weather, Fort Lauderdale was almost a complete opposite of Southern California. It was a quiet community with none of the show-biz flash of Los Angeles. Here Jimmy could be as private a person as he wished. There were no young people parading their movie-star parents' names, there was no night life. There were many rich people, but money was not talked about or thrown around or used to "put down" other people.

In a way, it was almost like being in a tropical Belleville, and it was just what Jimmy needed. Jim Evert, Chris's father, was manager of Holiday Park, a public tennis facility where Jimmy could practice anytime. Also, Chris's family gave Jimmy a sense of belonging, an atmosphere in which he could be himself, a second home. The years in California had been busy and exciting, but they had also been difficult in many ways. This, now, was the time to stop for a while and catch up on all the simple pleasures he had been forced to give up for tennis.

While Jimmy lived in Fort Lauderdale, he was as close to the average American boy as any super-champion could ever be. He had his first steady girlfriend, and they dated in a very un-Hollywood way. A typical evening meant a movie (never X-rated) and a bite to eat at a local hamburger restaurant or just sitting around the Evert house for an evening of television or listening to records. On Sundays Jimmy went to mass with the Evert family, who were devout Catholics and serious about church attendance.

Along with being a boyfriend to Chris, Jimmy could help her with her tennis. The role of instructor was new to him and must have been very enjoyable. The couple would spend about one hour every day playing together on the courts. First they might hit ground strokes, switch to lobs and dropshots, and then work on serve and return. Even though she was as much a champion as he, the benefits of their practice went more to Chris than to Jimmy. He could hit the ball harder than any woman she could face in a tournament; he could run farther, faster, and longer; he could return anything she hit at him.

Chris's main problem was her serve, which was too soft and predictable. Jimmy, who had worked hard on his own serve during his time in California, helped her put some spin and power into hers. Over and over Chris would serve to Jimmy, and he would show her, while returning it with ease, how she should sharpen it. Meanwhile, though he might not have realized it, he was reinforcing his own lessons every time he put his ideas into words for her. Also, when Chris did get over a good serve, it gave him a chance to work on his own game of placement, timing, and court strategy.

The contrast of their personalities was very interesting and valuable to both of them. Jimmy had the ability to cut through a tense moment with a joke. Chris was always serious. While they worked on her serve, she often reacted to her own fluffs by getting tight and missing even more. It was a vicious cycle—the worse she did, the more anxious she became; and the more anxious she became, the worse she did. Jimmy, seeing the problem, would stop play for a minute. He'd take the ball and, like a clown, imitate her pitty-pat serve with great exaggeration. It never failed to break up Chris. Then, after she had recovered from the giggles, she could start again, relaxed. The lesson Jimmy was teaching was one he would remember in his own future matches: When you tighten up, you lose. So stay loose.

On the other hand, Jimmy had much to learn from Chris. Her serenity and quiet dignity, off court, were traits he could admire and copy. And on court the patience of her play provided another lesson. There were times, as Jimmy could see, when the best strategy was to slow down the game, go for long rallies, and let the opponent make the mistakes. This was the basic Evert style—machinelike precision combined with total and unwavering concentration. It didn't fit the overall pattern of play in men's tennis; but it could be used to break up the rhythm of a match, and that could win points.

Jimmy was showing Chris how to put some power and speed in her game. Chris was showing Jimmy how to use ground stroke rallies to slow down his game. And, during all those months of practice in Fort Lauderdale, Jimmy was falling in love.

Eventually, however, it was time to leave warm, peaceful Fort Lauderdale and get back to business. The 1973 winter indoor season was beginning, and Jimmy was ready to show the world he was better than ever. His chance came in the first week of the new year at the Baltimore Indoor Tennis Championship. It was Connors all the way. He beat Sandy Mayer—6–4, 7–5—for the singles title. Then he teamed with Clark Graebner to win the doubles.

As the indoor season began, Jimmy kept his winning form. Except for three losses, he emerged the champ in every tournament he entered. It was getting easy—maybe too easy—to nail the top prize. The European tour would be getting under way in the late spring, and a satisfied, relaxed Connors thought he was ready. This year he wouldn't be the green kid going over. This year everything, especially himself, would be different.

It was quite a group that traveled to Europe together: Jimmy, his mother, his manager, Chris Evert, and her mother. It was a warm, secure cocoon in which Jimmy felt very comfortable. Off court, he laughed and joked and went out with Chrissie. The bad boy image he had been stamped with seemed to be a mistake. He didn't scowl or make insulting gestures. He didn't allow hecklers to get under his skin. He didn't clown or make nasty remarks to anyone. This Jimmy Connors, observers noted, was a new, improved model.

There was only one problem. The new Jimmy Connors was playing mediocre tennis. He couldn't seem to pull himself into finals play. One after another of the European tournaments came and went, with Jimmy flubbing his chances.

At Wimbledon, while Chris made it to the finals (where she lost to Billie Jean King), Jimmy barely squeaked into the quarter finals. There, in a match distinguished mostly by its boredom, he lost to Alex Metreveli, of the USSR. Only in the doubles was he successful. Teamed with Rumania's Ilie Nastase, Jimmy showed some spark, as they beat Neale Fraser and John Cooper, of Australia, for the championship. This win was nice, but it wasn't the big one. The singles title carried the real glory and fame.

Everyone had a different theory about what was wrong with Jimmy. Some said that it was plain old second-year slump. Most players who started out with a bang went through this kind of letdown. It was normal. The first time out, nobody expected you to win. So every time you did you were a hero. Then you became the one to beat, and everyone was watching, while each opponent was keying in on you. Some athletes can't take the pressure and just quit the sport. Others suffer through the slump and come out stronger for it.

There were other theories about Jimmy. One was that he was a second-rate player who just didn't have it and had never been worth all the press he had received. Still another was that he didn't care enough about winning the big tournaments. And yet another was that he choked when the going got rough.

One tennis writer had the most interesting (and probably most accurate) explanation of all. "It's swell to see Connors being such a gentleman," he said, "but that is what's killing his game. Some guys need a total psych to be winners, and he's one of them.

"It may not be pleasant for others when Connors goes into his act," the man continued, "but that's their problem. He's just gotta do it. Like, long before a match, he thinks himself into a kind of anger, building up a sort of hate for the guy on the other side of the net. And by the time he goes out on the court Connors is a potential killer facing an enemy. He hits the ball as if he wants to destroy it; he uses psychological warfare against players, officials, fans. He becomes the lone cowboy in the movies, showing no mercy against all the bad guys. And that's when Connors wins.''

Then the writer said, "As soon as he figures out that the Evert style works for Chris but not for him, he'll be okay. He has to stick to what works for him, and that's the kill mentality. He'll realize it, and he'll be fine again. Believe me, when he does, he won't be liked. But his tennis will sure be respected.''

Back in the United States after his dismal European tour, Jimmy did return to his old ways—and to winning. It began with the U.S. Pro Championships, held at the Longwood Cricket Club, near Boston, Massachusetts, in July. Because Jimmy had spent the spring on a different tour from the other top pros, he was unseeded. He didn't let that rattle him. Nor was he bothered by the fact that his first match was against Stan Smith, who was seeded number one. The rankings were ridiculous, as he proved by stunning Smith in straight sets, 6–3, 6–3.

"I was psyched up for this tournament," Jimmy said, "because it was my first WCT event. Then playing Stan in the first round got me even higher, and I stayed that way. I wasn't mad about the seedings. I didn't play the WCT circuit, and they went by the points. You have to play the top guys sometime to win the tournaments, so what difference does it make? If I couldn't beat Smith in the first round, I didn't deserve to go any further.''

Jimmy was Mr. Tennis at Longwood, rolling over Ray Moore, Dick Stockton, and Cliff Richey and into the finals. There he was matched against Arthur Ashe, the tournament's second seed. It was a heck of a contest. For more than three hours they slugged it out. The first set went to Connors, 6–3. Ashe surged back to take the second, 6–4. Both pros were playing carefully yet powerfully, wary of each other's ability and finesse while leaping onto every opportunity to put the ball away for a point.

The match went on that way. Jimmy took the third set, 6–4. Ashe came back to even it at two sets apiece, winning the fourth by a 6–3 margin.

In the end it was Jimmy's superior firepower that did it. He bombarded Ashe in the fifth set, 6–2, wrapping up the championship and the $12,000 first-prize payoff.

Afterward the defeated Ashe said, "I've never seen a guy keep hitting so hard and deep for so long. He just kept pounding away. For one week he was in a class by himself."

Jimmy was walking on air. "I think that's the best I've ever played in my life," he said. Then, asked if he always hits shots so hard, he smiled and replied, "Yeah, but they don't always go in."

Luckily—or maybe skillfully—they continued going in. Later that month he downed Charles Pasarell in the finals of the Buckeye tournament, 3–6, 6–3, 6–3. On into September, when he swamped Tom Okker in straight sets at the Pacific Southwest Open, bouncing back from Forest Hills, which had been a disappointment for Jimmy. There he had reached the semifinals, to find himself pitted against John New-combe. The match took two sudden-death tie break-ers, but Newcombe won both of them. And that was the difference.

In October Jimmy won the Rothman's Interna-tional, in Quebec, Canada. From there it was on to South Africa, for that country's Open, after a hop to Sweden. Jimmy was knocked out in the semifinals of the Swedish Open, but in Johannesburg, South Africa, he played the finals with absolute brilliance against Arthur Ashe. Jimmy trounced Ashe in straight sets, 6–4, 7–6, 6–3.

The Ashe-Connors set-to was an emotional one in many ways. First of all, with Stan Smith bogged down in an end-of-the-year slump, the spotlight had been focused on Jimmy and Arthur. They were the big guns on the tour. There was also the memory of their classic duel at Longwood and the prospect of another long, agonizing battle. But overshadowing all that was the simple fact that Arthur Ashe, a black man, was a finalist in a South African tournament, and South Africa was a very racist country. Jimmy wanted the win, but with honor to himself and no disgrace to Ashe. So Jimmy maintained a dignified silence, hoping the racial issue would take a back seat to the playing of a good match. But the pressure on Ashe was overwhelming, and his game fell apart. However, Ashe—always a gentleman—made the point that Jimmy was a fine person, had played great tennis, and deserved his win.

On Jimmy's side, there was equal politeness and understanding. "Arthur handled himself extremely well," he said. "But by the time we played he was bothered, and it showed on the court. That kind of thing is unfortunate. But I was playing well, and I like to think I could have beaten him regardless of the circumstances."

This was a kind of poise and self-assurance Jimmy had never shown before. He had not been capable of such a sensible, well-balanced attitude a couple of years before. And so it seemed fitting that when he returned from South Africa, the big announcement was made. Jimmy Connors and Chris Evert were engaged to be married. The wedding would take place soon, sometime before the 1974 European season.

But almost immediately, wiser and less emotional arguments were presented to the young couple. It's all very well to be engaged, they were told, but reason argued against rushing into marriage. As Gloria Connors was reported to have said, "No way anybody wins Wimbledon on their honeymoon."

Jimmy had faced his slump head-on and come through victorious. He was co-holder of the number one ranking in the United States with Stan Smith, and he knew that a few solid wins would give him sole ownership of the top ranking. And so he agreed with the adult advice—his private life would have to wait while he poured himself, body and soul, into tennis.

8

"The Mean Machine"

It could have come from the corniest movie script ever written. Jimmy Connors and Chris Evert, Wimbledon champions, the two hottest tennis players in the world, were going to be married after all. How could anything be more perfect? The story had everything—youth, success, suspense, romance.

The wedding was still "go" when Jimmy returned to the United States after winning Wimbledon. Then reality began to lean heavily on the dream. And the reality made itself clear even as the marriage plans were set for November, and both families were preparing for a church wedding in Fort Lauderdale. Jimmy should have been around, helping make the plans and decisions that go with a marriage, and so should Chris. Except that Jimmy was hopping around the country on the men's tour, and Chris was traveling in another direction on the women's circuit. The best they could do was communicate by phone and, when their schedules allowed it, grab a day now and then to be together. It was a miserable way to be engaged and no way to prepare for a wedding.

Publicly, things were smooth. Underneath, there were problems. With their tours keeping them apart, when would they be a couple? Which one should give up some tennis to be with the other? Should one of them retire, or both, for the sake of a marriage, a home?

Both Jimmy and Chris wanted to continue their careers. Both felt it would be wrong to ask the other to make sacrifices. Both were mixed up and unhappy about the situation, but they put off the problem until after Forest Hills. Now was the time to pay strict attention to tennis.

Jimmy wanted the U.S. Open crown. After Wimbledon that title held the most prestige. So he planned his summer with this in mind. It needed the right balance: not too many summer tournaments, to avoid being tired and stale; not a complete rest either, or he'd be out of shape. As the summer moved along, Jimmy began to gear up. In August he entered the U.S. Clay Court Championship, in which he was top seed. This would show whether Wimbledon had been a fluke or whether he deserved to be considered the world's best.

It was a breeze for Jimmy, all the way to the finals. But here he had to cross rackets with Bjorn Borg, the fast-rising, eighteen-year-old Swedish phenom. Borg was a master on clay, a deadpan, machinelike stroker who never let up. As the match began, it looked as if it would be another snap for Jimmy, that Borg wasn't quite ready for him. Then the unsmiling teenager began to take one point after another. The first set had been 5–2 in Jimmy's favor when Borg started his comeback. Five games later Borg locked up the set, 7–5.

Jimmy toweled off and thought hard about the upcoming second set. It was still anybody's match, and he was determined to turn the tide back in his direction. Borg was equally determined, and the score stayed even for a while, neither player able to break through the other's game. Then, at 2–2, Jimmy put it all together. Driving Borg from one corner to the other, making him sweat for every shot, Jimmy whipped him in three straight games and thundered on to win the set, 6–4. Now they were even, but Jimmy had the momentum.

The third set was a repeat of the second. It was double-barreled tennis—no brilliant, crowd-awing strokes, just a lot of long rallies and careful placements. But Jimmy outdid Bjorn in patience and skill, taking the final set, 6–4, and with it the $16,000 first prize.

One more major tournament to go before Forest Hills. That was the Eastern Grass Court Championship, to be held in South Orange, New Jersey. It was important because it was on grass, which was the surface at the Open. With fewer and fewer grass courts in the country, there were not many places players could prepare for Forest Hills. The Eastern was the traditional warm-up, and it gave tennis fans a pretty good preview of what was to come.

Jimmy was "up" for this one, planning to flash through South Orange and on to Forest Hills. And it looked as if everything would work just that way, at least until the final match. Then trouble struck, and it had nothing to do with tennis. Jimmy was sick, and he had to default to Alex Metreveli. The illness might have been caused by a virus because Jimmy suffered terrible stomach pains. It was also a little scary since it wasn't the first time something like this had happened to him. The year before there had been a rumor that Jimmy had an ulcer brought on by the mounting tension of competition. Now the whispers began to circulate again—that Jimmy's stomach trouble was a nervous condition; that things were sour with Chris; that he was choking up before a key competition and calling it illness.

But when the U.S. Open began, there was Jimmy, healthy and eager to play. Obviously the rumors had been empty ones. It *had* been a simple stomach virus, nothing more. Still, the promoters didn't want to risk losing their biggest draw to illness, and they delayed Jimmy's opening match for one day.

This pleased Jimmy immensely. "That extra day will allow me to come in strong," he said. "I've won Wimbledon, and now I'd like to win Forest Hills. I don't say I will, but I'm ready."

The promoters' decision touched off cries of "favoritism" and accusations that they were more interested in dollars than fairness to *all* the players. Jimmy wished that people would "lay off," that they would stop paying so much attention to his health and other outside matters and just concern themselves with how he played tennis. He especially wanted them to keep their noses out of his private life. It hurt him that other players actually wanted bad things to happen to him, that they were jealous of his success and said mean things about him to reporters. Jimmy was bitter.

"What are friends?" he asked after the press released a particularly harsh blast at him. "People who like you for what you are and who you like for what they are. I have Chrissie and her family. Pancho Segura and his family. Pancho Gonzales and his family. Bill Riordan and his family. And my family. What else do I need? I'd rather have a dozen good friends than a hundred who stab you in the back."

This statement only added fuel to the fire. A number of players, who felt that Jimmy's own behavior was at fault, completely refused to have anything to do with him. Others just plain bad-mouthed him. That added to Jimmy's belief that they were against him, every one, and got him angrier. By the time Forest Hills began he was worked up to a fine fury. Even his coaches, the two Panchos, wouldn't have described him as a nice person at that moment. He was, in their words, "vicious" and "nasty mean." But that was exactly what Jimmy had to be to win.

When Jimmy walked out onto the court for his opening match, against Jeff Borowiak, it was like a gladiator entering an arena full of lions. The crowd was there to see him lose, and they made no attempt to hide their feelings. Under a gray, rain-threatening sky, Jimmy took his place at one end of the court. He paced back and forth impatiently. He'd show 'em.

In the first two sets Jimmy played his usual style of steady tennis, winning tennis. He wasn't blowing his opponent away, but that didn't matter. He was winning the key points. The first and second sets were his, 6–3 and 6–4. Just one more set, and he'd advance into the next round.

The already-leaden sky grew even darker, and a slight drizzle began. The grass grew slick under the players' feet. The ball sponged up the wetness with every bounce, getting heavier. Jimmy was moving cautiously now, conserving his strength. Borowiak shifted to the attack. It was his last shot at staying in the tournament, and he gave it everything he had.

It was a strategy that made good sense. Connors had to save something for later matches against the really tough players. Borowiak would be like a giant killer if he won just this one, even if he were eliminated in the second round. He'd be the man who scored an upset over the champ, like the nobody who shoots the famous gunslinger and makes his reputation.

Jimmy seemed tired in the third set, and his play faltered. Then, with Borowiak leading 5–3, a heavy rain began, interrupting the match. Both players scurried to the locker room to change into dry clothes and wait for the storm to pass. Jimmy sat by himself, drinking tea with lemon, and tried to keep his mind on the contest. If he held his concentration, the rest period would give him a chance to come back and take the match. But if his mind eased up, no amount of rest would help.

When play resumed, Connors was back in the groove. Borowiak took the third set, 6–3, winning the one game he needed. But that was it for him. Jimmy won the fourth set, the deciding one, 7–5, to clinch the match. He'd let everyone know it wasn't so easy to take out the champ.

Asked whether he had been worried by Borowiak or upset by the rain, Jimmy said, "The weather today was Wimbledon weather. I don't mind it. I'm loose now. I just enjoy it out there. I play the game the way it should be played." Nobody disagreed with that statement.

Connors' next match, in which he beat Alex Metreveli, proved it again. And now he had to face Jan Kodes, of Czechoslovakia, in the quarterfinals. This one promised to be more of a tussle since Kodes had as much power and pace as Jimmy. An even duel was predicted by the experts. Jimmy had other plans.

The first and second sets went to Connors so easily (7–5 and 6–3) that the crowd began to look bored. And when Jimmy broke Kodes' serve in the first game of the third set, the fans were getting ready to leave. Kodes, however, was not ready to give up. He started mixing up his shots, hitting harder and deeper, going for killers. Slowly, the score evened, went against Connors, and Kodes took the set, 7–5.

This was more like it, the applause of the spectators seemed to say. They all settled back, expectant, as the fourth set got under way. Jimmy, appearing unruffled by the surprising turn of events, had service in the first game. His serves were hard and true, but the Czech's returns were better, and he won the first game. Jimmy played his game well, but it wasn't enough to stop the inspired Kodes. The Czech held his serve, making the score 2–0 in his favor.

In the third game Connors, ignoring the cheers of the crowd as they encouraged his opponent, came raging back. He held serve, bringing the score to 2–1, then captured the fourth game, tying it up. Jimmy had hit his stride, and as hard as Kodes tried, the Czech couldn't win another game. Wrapping up the fourth set, 6–2, Jimmy moved into the semifinals.

As Jimmy edged closer to the crown, the tension kept building. Bill Riordan, his manager, began to talk about the finals even before Jimmy played his semifinal match. "This is the best tennis I have ever seen him play," Riordan said after the win over Kodes. "Jimmy didn't play this well at Wimbledon until the finals."

Others were less certain of Connors' chances. "It

is almost impossible for one player to win all the big tournaments," Ilie Nastase explained. "It becomes important for a good player to win one of them. Jimmy has already won Wimbledon." Pressed to make a prediction, Nastase refused. Instead, he said, "Just before Wimbledon, Jimmy said to me, 'I don't think I can win.' But he did win because he was good and he was lucky, too. If you are not lucky, you can't win." It seemed Nastase didn't think Jimmy's "luck" would hold up.

Connors needed some of that luck in his semifinal tilt against Roscoe Tanner because he wasn't playing his usual sharp game. And Jimmy *was* lucky—because his opponent was even more off his game. Tanner had blasted his way into the semis on the strength of serves that hummed at better than 100 miles an hour, sizzling ground strokes, and deadly volleys. But he must have used up most of them.

The first two sets were decided by tie breakers, after reaching 6–6. And both times Jimmy won the sudden-death segments, 5–2. That made it 7–6, 7–6, Connors. The third set saw better play from both ends of the court, but that didn't change the outcome as Jimmy closed it out with a 6–4 win.

The after-match press conference was very subdued. "Roscoe was serving bombs all week," Jimmy told reporters, "but today he served a lot of spin and slice. He had an unbelievable tournament, but I guess he was a little tired." Jimmy was modest about himself, complimentary to his beaten opponent, and didn't once brag the way the newsmen expected him to.

Tanner, however, said, "Connors will have to play a lot better against Kenny tomorrow if he's going to win."

Kenny. Ken Rosewall vs. Jimmy Connors in the finals. The two men who had gone against each other two months earlier in the championship match at Wimbledon. Rosewall, the thirty-nine-year-old Australian, who had lost to Jimmy in a very fast ninety-three minutes. There would be drama on the Forest Hills court.

Jimmy's confidence was way up. "I feel loose as a goose," he said. "No pressure on me, I'm eager."

Rosewall, who had displayed top-level tennis all through Forest Hills, was philosophical. "I wonder how much longer it's going to last," he said. "I'm playing the type of tennis that will win a lot of matches. I'm still putting my game on the line, just like everybody else."

It was a massacre. The first set took only nineteen minutes, with Rosewall going through the motions like a weary, worn warhorse. Jimmy played with the energy and dash of a fresh, young colt. The score, 6–1, didn't come close to telling the story. Including the game he won, Rosewall took only 12 points in the entire set. The fans, in shocked silence, hardly moved in their seats.

It was Jimmy's serve to begin the second set. This

time the score shifted back and forth. At 30–40, Rosewall's favor, the Australian had the opportunity to pull himself back into the match by breaking Connors' serve. But the American had the magic touch once more and won the point. Deuce. Again the gutsy veteran dug down and produced a smasher that gave him the advantage. And again he needed just one point for the game. This was the drama people had come to see, and many of them were rooting for the underdog.

Connors served fast and hard. Rosewall moved toward the ball, reached it. But his return was weak and landed in the net. Deuce. Twice more, like a filmstrip being rerun, Jimmy served and conquered. The first game of the second set was his.

The whole set, in which Rosewall failed to take one game, lasted twenty minutes. Ilie Nastase, watching the match, shook his head in wonder. "Jimmy hits the ball so hard now," he said. "Unbelievable. Incredible."

As the players took their places for the third set, Jimmy was aware of the emotional waves that were coming from the spectators. Overwhelmingly the feeling was for Rosewall and against him—for the old man being taken apart and against the kid doing it. Even so, Jimmy refused to let his concentration— and his attack—waver for one second.

"I've seen people pity Ken Rosewall," Jimmy said afterward, "and then see him win six-three in the fifth. In the back of my mind I held the thought that if I let down, Rosewall could win it. My heart was going boom-boom against my shirt. I was afraid I'd come down. I had to keep the pressure on."

In the third set Rosewall clawed back like a wounded animal, making Jimmy labor for his points. Four games went to deuce before Jimmy could take them. One game saw Rosewall playing with the flash of youth Jimmy had worried about. But it was only a flicker of strength, a brief flame that glowed and went out. And then it was as good as over. Time after time Rosewall was caught flat-footed, caught helplessly in mid-court, while Jimmy zinged over beautiful two-handed backhand whistlers, low forehand ground strokes. One by one they passed the old warrior—as time had—landing on the chalk, in the corners.

Connors closed the set at 6–1. He was the U.S. Open king, and he'd done it in express-train time— sixty-eight minutes.

Rosewall, always a gentleman, smiled and congratulated the champion. It wasn't easy to be a gracious loser, especially since the match had been such a one-sided affair. But Rosewall was up to it, even though, as Nastase said, "You know, when you lose like that, you are like naked in front of all the world."

Jimmy was jubilant in victory. "It's the best tennis I've ever played in my life, all twenty-two years of it," he said. "I didn't miss a ball. When I played in the final at Wimbledon, I thought that was the best I could ever play. But I was really better today."

Jimmy hoped that at last he'd be accepted on his merit. He was the greatest player in the world, having taken the two highest tournaments. If Wimbledon hadn't proved it, Forest Hills had. And if even that didn't convince the doubters, he was ready to take on every ranking player on earth to make believers of them all.

9

Jimmy Connors vs. the World

During the Forest Hills finals while Jimmy was crushing Ken Rosewall into the dust, a fan had yelled out, "Connors, you're a bum!" Jimmy, getting set to serve, gazed up at the stands and grinned. "I agree," he called back.

Sometimes it seemed as if Jimmy *wanted* to be known as the meanest guy on earth. He screamed at officials in the middle of a match, talked back to insulting fans (trying to outdo their profanity), made obscene gestures, threw his racket when he didn't like a call, and developed a whole set of stalling tactics. At the same time he was racking up tournaments all over the place, destroying his opponents, proving that everyone else was at least a notch below him on the tennis scale.

Why, when he was so superior on the court, did he bother with the antics that made him so unpopular? Everyone had an opinion. Marty Riessen, who had been Jimmy's doubles partner more than once, said, "Jimmy is really kind of fun, kind of childlike. Oh, he does a lot of annoying things, but I think that's just immaturity.

"I think he has some very good qualities," Riessen continued. "Some things I like very much about him off court. Sally [Mrs. Riessen] and I asked him to stay over once at our place. He was very polite and courteous. And he made up his bed in the morning. That's a minor thing, but it shows he has consideration for his hosts. And in no situation where a woman was present has he ever been impolite or said anything embarrassing when I was around."

Stan Smith, with whom Jimmy had shared top ranking the year before, said, "Basically, Jimmy is a pretty good guy. He has the tendency to bounce the ball a lot, which annoys a lot of guys. But I think that's just his habit of doing things."

Tom Okker was less accepting of Jimmy's court conduct. "I don't like it," Okker said, "when you take five minutes to serve, and then you bounce the ball fifteen times and blow on your hand. Jimmy's still a child. I don't think the guys like him very much. When you're looking for someone to go to dinner with, he's not the first guy you ask. Jimmy is still very immature. He probably doesn't realize the way he acts."

And then Rod Laver, the great Australian pro, put in his opinion. "As a tennis player," Laver said, "Jimmy is just a little bit cocky. I think he's a good player, but being just a good player doesn't make you a champion. You don't know how to handle success when you're immature.

"Once," Laver went on, "Connors was playing

one of the Amritraj brothers at Mount Washington, and you had two players the same age but with such different attitudes that it was unreal. Amritraj would smile and acknowledge a good shot. The crowd was almost booing Connors for his actions. He's a very enthusiastic player, but that enthusiasm needs to be channeled in the right direction. I think he probably thinks he is the next best thing since Seven-Up.''

All these things had been said before Jimmy won Wimbledon and Forest Hills in 1974. He hadn't bothered to respond, except to make some acid remarks about friendship. Nevertheless, he was hurt and angry, especially at Laver's statement. They had never played each other (Laver having skipped Wimbledon and the U.S. Open), and Jimmy felt that the line about Seven-Up was an undeserved put-down.

So it was no surprise that after he won at Forest Hills, Jimmy turned to Bill Riordan and said, ''Get me Laver!'' At least that's the story that went around, and Jimmy never denied it.

Right from the start it was planned as a spectacular event. The idea was to stage Connors vs. Laver in October, at New York City's Madison Square Garden, the scene of so many heavyweight fights, championship basketball and hockey games, and the circus. They wanted the Garden because this tennis confrontation was expected to be in that category— big names, big money, big excitement.

Laver liked the idea of a match, but not in October.

"There's no way I'm going to play," he declared, "without going into training." At thirty-six years of age, Laver wanted to get in some challenging tennis before going against Jimmy. So the date was put off into early 1975.

Meanwhile, Jimmy was out on the tour, adding to his winnings (to reach a total of $286,000 for 1974). His engagement to Chris Evert had been broken just after Forest Hills, and he had plenty of time for tennis without any distractions. The sport was what counted most in his life now.

As 1974 ended, Jimmy was in Australia for that country's Open. Many pros didn't take the trouble to enter that one, because it was held during the Christmas-New Year's holidays, and they wanted to be with their families. But Jimmy had his mother and Spencer Segura with him in Australia, so he didn't feel lonely.

All the young Australian players were gung-ho to play Jimmy, each vowing to be the one to knock him out of the tournament. Jimmy was calm about it. "I don't care how many there are," he said. "Bring them on one after another. I'll beat them all."

The only player who roused Jimmy's interest was John Newcombe, whom the Australians regarded as their ace and who had accused Connors of ducking him. To this charge, Jimmy replied, "Newcombe should do more talking with his racket and less with his mouth. He says I've been ducking him, but I don't need to duck anybody. Every time I reach a final, he's missing." It was shaping up into an old-fashioned grudge match.

As the two stars won their way up through the elimination rounds, anticipation mounted. And when Connors and Newcombe made it to the finals, the showdown attracted the largest crowd ever assembled for tennis in Australia in twenty years. It was a pro-Newcombe group, ready to cheer for their countryman and to boo the Yank who sometimes behaved so badly and always played so brilliantly.

Jimmy felt cool and at the top of his game. In the five matches he played to reach the finals, he had lost only one set. Newcombe had played some grinders, including a five-set semifinal against Tony Roche, in 95-degree heat. He was tired, and he wasn't going to take any chances. As part of his preparation for the title match, Newcombe watched Jimmy's other matches on TV and planned a strategy. "You have to know how to serve to beat Connors," he said. "Serving to Jimmy is like pitching to Hank Aaron. If you don't mix up your stuff, he'll hit it out of the ball park. He's strong from the service line, but he's got certain weaknesses in his volley. He doesn't disguise his shots, except for his lob. He relies on his power stroke and the brute strength of his forehand. And on his second serve he likes to stay back, because he's not sure of it."

Newcombe not only had a strategy, but followed it right down the line. He threw in a lot of volleys, and

Jimmy's weakness showed. The first set wasn't a wipeout for the American, but for the first time in the tournament he was on the defensive. The score: Newcombe, 7, Connors, 5.

While the players were walking off the court for a brief break before the second set, a spectator yelled to Connors, "What happened, Mouth?" Jimmy didn't even acknowledge that he heard it.

The second set began. Connors was serving. With none of his infamous antics, just good tennis, Jimmy took the first game. The audience was very quiet as Newcombe set to serve for the second game.

Jimmy bent into his swaying crouch. His racket, held loosely in both hands, was pointed across the net like a rifle aimed at his rival. Then came the serve, a grunting slammer. Jimmy moved into return position swiftly. With his two-handed backhand grip, he looked like a batter with a wide-open stance, waiting for the pitch. Then, boom! Connors' return was like a line drive hammered through the infield. Newcombe was flung back on the defensive now, forced to play Jimmy's style and not able to. Jimmy, coming in behind his magnificent return of service, set the tune and made Newcombe dance to it, breaking the Australian's serve.

Jimmy held his service in the third game, bringing the score to 3–0. The fans shouted encouragement to Newcombe, hoping that he'd get back in his first-set groove. And their man won the next game, but Jimmy still had the momentum. The Australian tried to break Jimmy's serve and couldn't. The score, with Jimmy always holding the lead, went 3–1, 4–1, 4–2, 5–2, 5–3, 6–3. The set was Jimmy's, and the fans showered him with abuse.

All along, however, something strange was happening, and the crowd didn't seem to notice. Jimmy Connors, the bad boy of the international tennis circuit, wasn't answering the remarks thrown at him, wasn't making gestures at the hecklers or officials. He was behaving exactly the way his critics said he should—and nobody was paying attention to his good behavior.

In the third set, with Newcombe ahead, 3–2, Jimmy had the serve. The first point went to Newcombe on a blasting volley: 0–15. Connors bounced the ball, swaying with the rhythm of the bounce, lofted the ball, and served. Newcombe's return was in, but right into Jimmy's backhand, which sent the ball into the opposite corner of the court. The call on Jimmy's shot gave him the point, tying the score at 15–all. The spectators began hooting and whistling—they had seen it go out or wanted to influence the linesman to change his call.

On the next serve there was another contested call which went to Connors, making it 30–15, Jimmy's favor. As Newcombe stood there, shaking his head (though not complaining about the call), the local fans roared their disapproval. The situation began to look ominous, as if the whole arena were on the edge of an explosive riot. And Jimmy, if anyone bothered to check, just looked worried.

When Jimmy's next serve, a zoomer, was called good by the linesman, the crowd burst into a fury. Newcombe groaned and stamped his foot either because he had lost the point on an ace or because he thought the serve had gone out. The officials stayed with the call (which really hadn't been *that* close), while the rumbling anger of the fans sent waves of hate at them and at Connors. It was an ugly, frightening moment.

The noise continued as Jimmy set to serve. Then, very obviously, he faulted on the serve. Could he be so shaken by the situation that he made a mistake? Then, on his second serve, when he faulted again, it was clear. Jimmy had deliberately double-faulted to give the point to Newcombe. The score had been 40–15. Now it was 40–30.

The fans gave no sign that they had noticed Jimmy's sacrifice. But John Newcombe did—by jumping on the advantage, bringing the score to deuce, and going on to take the game. It could have been 3–3. Jimmy's double fault and what followed made it 4–2. The rest of the set was hard, fairly even tennis, and Newcombe won it, 6–4.

Connors played strong tennis in the fourth set, but Newcombe was superb. The Australian's flaming serves, including two aces, made the score 5–3. But

Jimmy wasn't out of it yet. He came back to take the next game, making it 6–6 and forcing a tie breaker.

With the set on the line, Newcombe forged to a 4–1 lead, only to see Jimmy rally with solid ground shot and forehand placements that gave him the advantage at 6–5. One more point for Jimmy, and the set would be his. This time Newcombe, on the strength of his serve, evened it at 6–6. Again, Jimmy went ahead, 7–6, but that was his last gasp of the set. Newcombe posted three straight points to end it, 9–7. Game, set, and match to John Newcombe, the winner of the Australian Open.

After the traditional handshake Jimmy was asked about his polite, mild-manner behavior in the third set. "I don't regret double-faulting," he answered. "But from now on I'll be meaner. I don't ever want a crowd to put me in that situation again."

Had Jimmy been right to play the gentleman? All Newcombe had to say was: "I wouldn't have thrown the serve away like that for him."

A writer covering the Open heard Newcombe's statement and laughed. "It figures," he said. "Everyone's been working at Jimmy, trying to throw him off his game. They know that his silliness—the dirty remarks and the hand gestures—don't mean anything. They also know that the way to get at him is to break his concentration. You see, once the other players can get Jimmy thinking about what he should do *between* points, they keep him from focusing on his play. The others are no better than he is. You don't get to be a top pro by being a good guy who gives away points.

"Don't look for Jimmy to be conned again," the writer added. "He'll play to win from now on, and if that means going through his act for a psych-up, he'll do it. There's a story about a guy saying to his kid, 'Don't be afraid to jump off the ladder. I'll catch you.' So the kid jumps, and the guy lets him fall. When the kid asks why, the guy says, 'Now you know better than to trust anyone.' I'd say that's the lesson Jimmy Connors learned today."

10

The Match of the Century

The big buildup increased as the Connors-Laver match drew nearer. It was scheduled for Sunday, February 2, 1975, at Caesars Palace in Las Vegas, Nevada. There would be national TV coverage, a winner-take-all purse of $100,000, press conferences, lots of Hollywood stars on hand, and all the razzle-dazzle of a major sporting event.

The tennis establishment acted horrified. "I'd hate to see a trend start," said Jack Kramer, the former Wimbledon and Forest Hills champion who was now a tennis promoter. "It's just a way for a couple of guys to make a lot of money. What does it prove? Tennis is not like boxing or wrestling. The worst thing that could happen is that people could start making a lot of money without doing much. It would depreciate the real part of the game, which is tournaments." Of course, Kramer meant *his* kind of tournament.

Jimmy, having learned a thing or two in the Australian Open, shrugged when Kramer's comment was repeated to him. "I wonder what he would do in my position?" Jimmy mused. "And why did he have all those ten-thousand-dollar winner-take-all promotions years ago?"

Jimmy went on, "I think there is nothing better than winning a tournament. But tennis has become a very important thing in the world. People are living and breathing and playing tennis in great numbers. This is a new facet to it. It's like a heavyweight championship fight. I think people would like to see me against Nastase, or Nastase against Newcombe, and on and on. Keep the tournaments, yes. But what's wrong with throwing in a challenge match every now and then? Sure, it's a way to make money. But how many will watch us? Millions. They want to see us."

Of course, Jimmy was right—tennis was the fastest-growing sport in America, and people wanted to see head-to-head matches between well-known players. That was why more than 30,000 fans had been at the Astrodome to see Billie Jean King play Bobby Riggs in 1973, and millions more followed it on TV in fifty-seven countries. Tennis was no longer the private preserve of a few rich amateurs. Times were changing, and the sport had to change with them.

The groups which had always controlled tennis hated the idea of losing it—and the money involved—to newcomers. That was why World Team Tennis had been so opposed by the establishment groups. That was why Jimmy, who had joined WTT, had been barred from the French Open in 1974. And that was why there were as many lawsuits as tournaments in big-time tennis, and Jimmy had his share of them.

There also was the issue of the U.S. Davis Cup team, which Jimmy didn't join. When he refused the invitation, it was implied that he was un-American. But the people who ran tennis were the same ones who were involved in Davis Cup, and Jimmy wasn't about to knuckle under to them. Then, when the Davis Cup matches were scheduled for the same weekend as the Connors-Laver match, even some anti-Connors critics were forced to consider that he was being given a raw deal. Still, there were people—players and officials—who insisted that Jimmy should ask to be on the U.S. team, no matter how he was treated.

The only player with the guts to defend Jimmy in public was Billie Jean King, an independent scrapper herself. "I don't think he should play," Ms. King declared. "They [the selection committee] have treated him like a creep. You're not playing for the USA, but rather the USLTA. People should leave him alone. That's what this whole country is supposed to be about—freedom of choice. It's not Russia."

The setup was clear. If the Davis Cup team lost, the Establishment could say that it was because Connors had no national spirit. If the team won, it would show that Connors was unimportant. Either way he wasn't supposed to look good.

As far as Jimmy was concerned, the only thing that counted was his upcoming match against Laver. For that, he set up a training routine of diligent practice and plenty of sleep. As an added sharpener, he entered the Birmingham International Indoor Tennis tournament and won it easily. Immediately afterward he flew out to La Costa, California, to work out with Pancho Segura.

Rod Laver chose to go to Las Vegas early for his preparation. At thirty-six he felt the need for long and careful training. With Roy Emerson acting as his coach, and left-handed Mark Cox as his "sparring partner," every day was given to planning and trying out different shots and strategies. The odds favored Connors, because of his youth, and Laver knew it. Still, the experienced Australian thought he stood a good chance of taking the kid.

"It won't be as tiring as having to play several days in a tournament," Laver said, "and my experience should mean a great deal against Connors' youth. I am very happy with my form. I've been going four or five hours on a daily program because I feel my game needs that kind of work. My adrenaline is pumping hard."

Connors was equally confident about his own chances, but refused to say flat out that he'd win. "I predict this," he said with a smile, "it'll go three sets. If I wake up Sunday feeling good, watch out."

But before the big Sunday, there were things to be settled—what kinds of tennis ball to use, what the playing surface would be, and who would officiate. With as much seriousness as the representatives of two countries deciding war or peace, Connors' people and Laver's people met to negotiate. It seemed silly to outsiders, but it was all part of the buildup.

First, there was the matter of tennis balls. Jimmy had been under the impression that the match would be played with Dunlops, and so he was practicing with them. Then, when he got to Las Vegas, he learned that Laver was working out with Wilson heavy-duty balls and expected to compete with them. A minor disagreement, but Jimmy gave in—Wilsons it would be. Bill Riordan, Jimmy's manager, saw no problem. "Jimmy's grown up on Wilson balls, and I'm sure he can use them for the match."

Ah, but that didn't finish the game of one-upmanship. Laver now said that he wanted the cans of balls that were to be used on Sunday to be opened on Friday. This would take away some of their liveliness. Jimmy understood what Laver had in mind—slower, heavier balls would be to the advantage of the older player. Jimmy pointed out, however, that tournament tennis balls were always removed from the pressurized can right before a match. Laver's request, Jimmy's argument seemed to say, was as odd as opening a soda can two days before drinking the soda.

The disagreement was decided by a coin toss, which was won by Laver's side. The pressure would be off the balls on Friday.

The third problem was a pipe that ran the width of the court right under the net. The question was: If a ball slid over the net and hit the pipe, would it still be in play? Laver said yes, under some conditions. Connors said no, under any conditions. On this slight matter, Connors won.

The final item had to do with the officials. Laver wanted Pancho Gonzales, tennis director of Caesars Palace, as referee. Connors said no. Laver insisted. Connors said okay, but I pick the umpire and deputy referee. Laver agreed. And of course, the news media gave all this bickering broad coverage.

By the time everything was settled both sides could have qualified for the Nobel Peace Prize. But while everyone laughed at these prematch games, they knew that a real war, the one on the courts, would wipe all this from memory.

Sunday mornings in Las Vegas are usually quiet, but this one wasn't. In order to be on at prime viewing time in the East, the match was scheduled for 10 A.M., which would be 1 P.M. in the East. Everyone who could afford the price of a ticket—tickets went from $25 to $100—was there. Seated at courtside were Johnny Carson, Alan King, Charlton Heston, Clint Eastwood, Andy Williams, and dozens of other celebrities. As Connors had said, tennis was important in America.

Laver walked out onto the court, looking as sure of himself as if he were about to play an unranked novice. But underneath that outward calm, he had to be nervous—he had heard what other players were saying about Connors. Just a week earlier, Vitas Gerulaitis had said of Jimmy, "I saw him play a week or so ago, and he was hitting harder than last year. He's really hitting the ball so hard it's amazing. And it's *in* the court."

Then Ian Crookenden, who had worked out with Jimmy, said, "He's hitting about thirty percent harder and an inch closer to the line. His depth is incredible. He hits every shot so deep there's very seldom one short enough to move in on."

As the battle of the left-handers got under way, Laver continued to look cool and calm, while Jimmy seemed ready to jump out of his skin with eagerness. The younger man immediately set the pace, keeping his opponent back at the baseline. The play was attack for Jimmy, defense for Rod. Laver's serve (which had earned him the nickname Rocket) was still good enough to keep him going. But Jimmy's serves and two-handed hammer blows kept making the difference. The first set went to Connors, 6–4, and the second set was his, 6–2.

In the third set Laver delighted the crowd with an exhibition of the style that had made him a four-time Wimbledon champ. He was serving aces, crashing untouchable volleys, mixing up his shots, doing everything right, Jimmy fought on every point, but it was Laver's set, 6–3.

The fourth set, praised by many as the most memorable ever played in the entire history of tennis, was a long, bitter slugfest. The score reached 5–4, in Connors' favor, and it looked as if he had the match. Even though it was Laver's serve, Jimmy had a one-point edge and a psychological edge because he had the Australian on the brink of defeat. But Laver wasn't through.

Laver's legs were tired. Jimmy's nerves were twanging. And each time Rod would rocket one over the net, he'd be answered by one of Jimmy's crosscourt, tightly angled shots. The game went to match point, Connors. One more, and Jimmy would break Rod's serve. Laver refused to give ground, coming back once, then again, and again . . . five times in all, and tied the score at 5–5.

Connors held serve, to go up once more, 6–5. Was it almost over, or would the unyielding Aussie mount another comeback? Laver, wiping his face steadily, seemed ready to drop from exhaustion. And Jimmy seemed ready to begin a whole new match. And millions of people around the nation watched and waited. . . .

The last game, with Laver serving, went quickly, like a merciful death blow. The Australian didn't make a point. Connors had the shots and the luck to go with them. Twice the ball nicked the net and trickled over for winners for Jimmy. Both times Jimmy paused to gaze skyward and say something to himself. (He later revealed that he was saying, "Thank you, Grandma." He was sure Two-Moms was watching from up there.) And he won the set, 7–5, and the $100,000 payoff. He was a very happy young man.

It had been publicized as a winner-take-all match, but Laver collected $60,000 as the loser's share. And when he was asked if he'd be willing to play a rematch, he said, "Sure—if I get a year younger, I'll think about it."

Jimmy, showing none of the habits that had earned him the reputation of tennis' bad boy, had nothing but gracious compliments for Laver and modest pride in his own win. That made no difference to those who disliked Jimmy. All they talked about was that the U.S. Davis Cup team had been trounced by Mexico on the same weekend that Jimmy was earning so much money for himself.

If you didn't know that they were describing a tennis match, the press reports of Connors' defeat of Laver would have sounded like the description of a mugging. What's more, Jimmy's not playing Davis Cup was made to read as if he had stolen top secret documents and given them to a foreign power. No matter how Jimmy acted and no matter how often he won, his enemies refused to give him credit. And his popularity rating continued to sink.

Speaking for the minority (those who didn't equate Jimmy with Attila the Hun), Art Spander wrote in *The Sporting News*, "You might not get this idea from the people in the board rooms or locker rooms, most of whom appreciate Jimmy Connors about as much as the stomach flu, but Connors is the best thing to happen to American tennis in years. Maybe ever."

11

The New Jimmy Connors

For Jimmy Connors, 1975 was a year of great change. On and off the court. First, there was his famous romance with Chris Evert, which had ended in the fall of 1974. Jimmy, called Mouth by those who disliked him, refused to say anything publicly about it. And so few outsiders knew if Jimmy was hurt by the breakup or whether he or Chris had ended the engagement. All that was said was: Jimmy won't talk about it.

But early in the spring of 1975 the engagement was on again. It lasted until just before Wimbledon, when it was off again—this time, it seemed, for good. And the papers ran a few stories about the roller-coaster romance. Then Jimmy was photographed with other young women and, for the first time, began bringing dates to his tournaments. Even though he and Chris played doubles on the court, they remained separate off the court.

There was a "new" Jimmy Connors taking shape, a grown-up who wanted to take control of his own life. The lawsuits that had complicated his career were still hanging over his head and keeping teams of lawyers busy, but were coming closer to settlement. His relationship will Bill Riordan was thinning, but his friendship with fellow players was getting thicker.

His tennis year had begun with the smashing defeat of Rod Laver. Immediately arrangements were begun for a similar match with John Newcombe, winner of three Wimbledon and two Forest Hills championships and the man who had taken Jimmy in the Australian Open. Though Newcombe was thirty years old to Jimmy's twenty-two and a half, the Australian was still in top tournament condition. He had won the World Championship of Tennis final in 1974, and his prize money for the year had been about $250,000, not much less than Jimmy's. So this match shaped up as a good one. It was scheduled for the middle of April, at Caesars Palace in Las Vegas.

Both players went into training for the big confrontation. Newcombe used the two-on-one system, playing practice sessions against two opponents at the same time. That way he had to run all over the court to get at shots, just as he expected to against Jimmy. He also worked on lobs and soft shots— strokes that might force Jimmy to come in rather than play his choice of long, needle-threading ground strokes. Newcombe was leaving nothing to chance.

There was a tournament in Denver one week before the big match, and Newcombe, anxious to get in some last-minute sharpening, entered it. Then Jimmy decided to enter it, too, and the result was like an earthquake. CBS, which was to televise the Las Vegas match, was furious. NBC, which was carrying the Denver event, was delighted at the prospect of a Newcombe-Connors final that would make the challenge match an anticlimax.

Rod Laver, who had a good shot at winning in Denver, called Jimmy "a spoiled brat." And a number of other players, whose chances of success depended on Jimmy's staying away, were equally angry. All in all, it was quite an uproar.

Jimmy found the whole thing amusing, especially when Newcombe decided to default from the tournament. It was now, as Jimmy put it, "thirty-one losers and me"—a remark that made the other players even angrier. Their response led Jimmy to declare that he'd gladly buy every loser a pair of Haggars (that being the name of the brand of slacks manufactured by the tournament sponsor). When the Haggar people learned of Jimmy's statement, they had a most interesting reaction. "We've been sponsoring WCT for two years," a company official said, "and none of these turkeys has mentioned our name yet. I'm sending Connors a dozen pairs."

It isn't known whether Jimmy ever received the slacks, but he did win the Denver tournament, beating Brian Gottfried in the finals, 6–3, 6–4. And then, smiling the smile of a winner, he flew to Las Vegas for his meeting with Newcombe.

Like the Laver match, this one was preceded by a barrage of publicity and squabbling. There was big money involved (the winner would get from $500,000 to $1,000,000, the loser would get about $300,000, and CBS would get a high viewer rating and lots of advertising dollars), so all the participants welcomed publicity of any kind.

There was an argument about the playing surface (Newcombe won that one on a coin toss) and sniping remarks hurled back and forth for the benefit of the newspapers. Jimmy complained that, at the Laver match, the courtside had been packed against him with Laver fans. This time he wanted to buy 536 tickets to balance the rooting. His request was refused—it was pointed out to him that the hostility of the fans didn't stop him from beating Laver.

At last, it was Saturday, April 26, the day of the challenge match between the two best tennis players on earth, John Newcombe and James Scott Connors. And then it began, with millions of viewers watching every swing of the racket, every bounce of the ball.

In the first set, with his incomparable return of service, Jimmy took command. If Newk was to have a chance, he had to hold service—it was his one *must*. But Jimmy was slamming Newk's serves back into the Australian's midsection or at his feet. And each time Newcombe was thrown off-balance as he moved away to get some swinging room. The score jumped to 3–1, Connors, and he was an odds-on favorite to take the set. All he had to do was hold his own service. He did just that, wrapping up the set at 6–3.

Newcombe came back, his magnificent serve-and-volley game winning him the second set, 6–4. But that turned out to be his last gasp. Jimmy took charge again and wound up the match, 6–2 and 6–4. It was more like a Connors exhibition than a challenge match—the baseline ground strokes that darted into faraway corners; the aggressive two-fisted cannon-balls that slanted crosscourt to land near the net and scoot past the sideline; the serves as wicked and tricky as a pitcher's spitball.

Jimmy's triumph was a thing of beauty, and when reporters asked the defeated Newcombe if Connors was the best, the Australian answered, "I don't think you can dispute that now."

The rest of the year was an odd one for Jimmy. He made a pile of money on the pro circuit, but he lost the two big titles of tennis—Wimbledon and Forest Hills—and seemed to be losing the raging aggressiveness that had made him so exciting to watch.

The loss in the Wimbledon finals, to Arthur Ashe, 6–1, 6–1, 5–7, 6–4, brought no excuses from Jimmy. "Any guy has to play out of his mind to beat me," he said. "And Ashe beat me today." Then he added, "I walked in here with my head high. I walk out with my head high. And I'll be back here next year, and my head will be even higher." Let the Connors haters say what they wished, he was going to keep his dignity.

The story at Forest Hills was slightly different. Since the 1974 tournament, the playing surface had been changed from grass to a claylike composition. One by one, the Americans (more accustomed to faster surfaces) were knocked off. Out of forty-six Americans in the draw, only four went as far as the fourth round, and three of those (Ashe, Eddie Dibbs, and Harold Solomon) were finished before the semifinals. Clearly, the Europeans and South Americans, used to clay, had an advantage.

The semis saw Manuel Orantes of Spain defeat Guillermo Vilas of Argentina, and Jimmy beat Bjorn Borg of Sweden. One American left of forty-six, and it was Jimmy Connors, the defending champion. His opponent in the finals, Manuel Orantes, was a surprise contestant for the title. He had *never* won a major tournament and was almost unknown in this country. But those who knew of him also knew that he could be dangerous on clay—as Jimmy found out too late. This was a match of Orantes' soft, looping shots and patient game against Jimmy's take-the-ball-on-the-rise smashes. Patience won, 6–4, 6–3, 6–3.

After the Forest Hills loss, it seemed reasonable to expect that Jimmy's critics, who had made so much noise, would shut up and go away. But it wasn't that way. The fury and bile that poured out were sickening. "Connors is hardly a champion," one reporter wrote. "He has lost every final that really mattered this year." Another kicked Jimmy in print by saying, "It's hard to root against a guy from your own country. But, in a match with Connors, I'd root for anyone short of Hitler to beat him. I must say, I really enjoyed Forest Hills this year." And compared to some other comments, these were mild!

At the same time, while the press was getting in its barbs at Jimmy, player sentiment was growing more pro-Connors. Partly it was because all the lawsuits were being settled out of court, partly because a more mature Jimmy was behaving better, and partly because he was going to play Davis Cup for the United States.

Jimmy's one condition for playing Davis Cup— that Dennis Ralston not be captain—had been met by the USTA (this was the new name of the USLTA, with the L for Lawn removed). With Tony Trabert, a tennis champion of the 1950s, as the new captain, Jimmy was eager to join the team. He even said the things nobody had ever expected him to say, such as, "It's great to be playing for two hundred and ten million Americans instead of just Jimmy Connors," and "It's super to be here with these guys, helping each other in a team atmosphere."

When the team assembled in Tuscon, Arizona, in

October, for its series of matches against Venezuela, the others players got a huge shock. It wasn't on court (where they did well), but within their own team. Jimmy Connors, whom they had all thought of as the big bad wolf, was a decent human being. Suddenly player after player said it—that Jimmy was a nice guy. "Whatever you write about Jimmy here," Erik Van Dillen told a reporter, "write something good. He's really made an effort and worked his tail off. I think he has learned, just as in business, that you can't work a guy over and then expect him to have lunch with you, and a tennis player can't be an ass on court and a pal off the court.

"Segura once told me," Van Dillen continued, "that Jimmy hated me. But I didn't really know the kid. I'd see him at tournaments and say, 'Hi, good win,' or something. Now I don't hesitate to ask him to lunch or to go out on the town at night. That's what Davis Cup competition does to us guys."

Jimmy, needless to say, was very happy about his new acceptance. He, too, had learned something. During his years on the circuit he had been a loner and tightly protected by his own entourage. When there were decisions to be made, his people had made them. When statements had to be given to the press, his people had given them. But he was twenty-three years old now, and it was time to do it all himself. When he was younger, it had been right for others to guide and direct, to let him concentrate on tennis alone. He couldn't blame them if he had continued to lean on them—that had been his choice. But now he was ready to make his own decisions, statements, and friends—and he found that the world wasn't such a hostile place after all. It had taken an awfully long hard time, but Jimmy was becoming a man.

It all came together in 1976. Although Jimmy was knocked out of Wimbledon by Roscoe Tanner, in the quarterfinals, there was no question that he was the greatest tennis player alive. As one sportswriter put it, "On a scale of one to ten, Jimmy Connors is an eleven."

12

Number One in the World

Jimmy spent the summer of 1976 winning tournaments and lots of money. Then came the one he wanted very much—Forest Hills. Long before the first round, players started battling it out, and it became clear that this was going to be a spectacle and a major sporting event that would be talked about for years to come. Those who remembered the quiet, sedate U.S. Nationals of the past were stunned by what tennis had become. Tickets were being "scalped" for the matches in which favorites would appear, there was special TV coverage every night during the tournament, and a total purse of $416,000 (the largest in history) was being offered. The tournament would fill twelve days and see 128 men and 96 women playing for the top prizes of $30,000. Actually, it would have taken much longer than twelve days, except that a number of matches were scheduled at night. Tennis had become the equal of the World Series, the NBA play-offs or the NHL play-offs. It was important and big business.

A favorite from the outset, Jimmy still had to face

an array of clay-court specialists, all of whom stood a good chance of upsetting him—with Manuel Orantes among them. The matches would not be walkovers, and the enormous amount of attention put on the 1976 Open would make each match even more tense, more difficult. The Jimmy Connors who, in the past, had reacted to spectators as if they were battling him on every point, now decided to play his game with no high jinks on the court. He'd keep his mind on tennis, nothing else. "The New York crowd is a difficult crowd for me to play in front of," he said. "These people are used to hockey, basketball, football. They come to see blood. I don't want to give them any of mine."

Jimmy's first match, on Wednesday, September 1, was against Bob Hewitt, a thirty-six-year-old with a steady game. After winning it, 6–3, 6–3, Jimmy said, "I have to give myself a shot at the title. It's a long shot, but I'm there." Plainly, the *new* Jimmy Connors preferred modesty to bragging.

Hewitt, after the defeat, felt that Connors was far more than a long shot for the title. "Jimmy's got it all," he said. "He's getting better depth and not making silly errors. He's got as good a game as anyone, and he's got a tremendous mind." The concentration was paying off.

The rest of the first day's action provided some surprises, with a pack of top-ranked players being eliminated. Among them were Harold Solomon, Vijay Amritraj, Colin Dibley, Phil Dent, and Erik

Van Dillen. Playing on clay did weird things to some players—the power hitters had a tendency to blast themselves right off the court and out of the competition. And playing for the best two out of three sets (the change had been made when the courts went from grass to clay) threw a number off their game. The final rounds would be scored for the best three out of five, but the trick was to last that long—not an easy trick to perform.

The second round saw a number of other favorites bite the dust—Arthur Ashe, Adriano Panatta, and Raul Ramirez, along with a group of relative unknowns. In the second category was Peter Fleming, a young man from New Jersey, who lost to Jimmy Connors, 6–1, 6–0.

Meanwhile, the headline story of the Open was Ilie Nastase, Jimmy's friend. Only the story wasn't about tennis; it was about behavior. Nastase, the guy who was said to have taught Connors all his antagonizing tricks, was acting like a maniac on the court. He screamed at fans and officials, hit balls at photographers, made obscene gestures, spat at his opponent, threw his racket at the stands, and cursed at everyone within hearing distance. It was a disgusting exhibition. And Jimmy, aware of what was going on, said nothing. Perhaps, seeing someone else do the things that turned off everyone from fans to players, made Jimmy realize how he looked to others. Perhaps he now understood some things he'd never understood before.

Steadily and efficiently, Jimmy beat Fred McNair, 7–5, 6–3, and Vitas Gerulaitis, 6–4, 6–3, 6–1, in the first of the final rounds. The match against Gerulaitis was one to test Jimmy's resolution of good behavior. Because his opponent was a local player, there was an unusual atmosphere for tennis. The stands were packed with New Yorkers rooting for "their" guy and goading Jimmy. But Jimmy refused to bite at their bait. He stuck to his tennis.

Afterward Gerulaitis, who had never before played Jimmy on clay, called him "the man to beat." Then he added, "Let's face it. Jimmy's ground strokes are as good as anybody's. And if he volleys as well as he did against me, who can beat him?"

While Jimmy was getting ready for his quarterfinal match against Jan Kodes, other highly ranked competitors were falling beside the roadside. Orantes beat Stan Smith; Bjorn Borg eliminated Brian Gottfried. It was getting tighter.

The Connors-Kodes match was the first one in the Open in which Jimmy really had to extend himself. It was a two-hour battle, with each player trying to establish a pace that would ensure victory. Kodes refused to serve until Jimmy stopped swaying in his crouch as he waited for the ball. And Jimmy, when it was his serve, methodically bounced the ball four times before slamming it into play. It was a question of whose nerves were stronger. Jimmy won. The final score was Connors, 7–5, 6–3, 6–1. So far Jimmy had not lost a single set in the tournament.

Kodes, unlike the others Jimmy had beaten, refused to admit that he had lost to a superior competitor. "Whenever I play Jimmy," Kodes complained, "I seem to get bad calls. The time is coming when all the Europeans will stop coming to play in the United States."

Jimmy was amused by this statement. "Are you kidding?" he said. "The support for me? Two years ago I played Ken Rosewall here, and I had eight people for me. That's pretty good support," he added sarcastically. "Let's put it this way: I'd hate to have to play Kodes in Czechoslovakia."

On Saturday, September 11, Jimmy played his semifinal match against Guillermo Vilas. The strategy, worked out with Pancho Segura, was simple: Hit the ball deep, and keep moving Vilas from one side of the court to the other. However, no strategy works unless it can be altered to suit changing circumstances and conditions. There was, as the match was about to begin, a strong, gusty wind blowing when Connors and Vilas stepped onto the court. And it would continue to swirl throughout the match.

It was this wind—as confusing as it was unexpected—that showed what an exceptionally skillful player Jimmy had become. He changed his entire game plan each time the players changed sides. When the wind was blowing toward him, Jimmy put everything he had into his strokes. "I just hit every ball a hundred miles per hour," he said. But when he shifted to the other side of the net, he shifted to "just meeting the ball and timing it." This ability to adapt to the unexpected, coupled with his crosscourt sizzlers, gave Connors the match in straight sets, 6–4, 6–2, 6–1. And it didn't hurt his chances in the least that Vilas didn't change *his* game in keeping with the effects of the wind.

Now Jimmy waited to see whom he'd have to play for the championship. The match to decide that question pitted Bjorn Borg against the Wild Rumanian, Ilie Nastase. This semifinal, eagerly awaited by tennis fans (and, some said, by fight fans), proved to be an odd contest. Nastase, who served six aces, didn't seem otherwise able to get himself up for the match. Borg, in his usual icy, methodical way, just took Nastase apart, 6–3, 6–3, 6–4. And the answer was: Connors and Borg for the championship.

It was a bright and clear Sunday, September 12, 1976. Perfect weather for sports. The men's final was slated for four o'clock. This would mean that, as in late-season baseball, the shadows would creep across the arena, steadily changing conditions. But the 16,253 fans at Forest Hills and the millions seated in front of their television sets wouldn't have cared if the match had been staged at midnight in the rain. This pairing had the makings of a historical clash.

Borg came into the Open as the winningest player—so far—in 1976, having taken the U. S. Pro and WCT titles and the Wimbledon crown. Connors, after a dismal Wimbledon, had been winning all summer, and he was ranked number one. Furthermore, in six previous meetings with Borg, Jimmy had won five.

Both players looked strong and confident as play began, but Jimmy seemed to have the edge. He was on the attack, ramming home winners—fourteen of them before play ended. But his Swedish opponent didn't crumble under the pressure. He kept at his brand of tennis, relying on long rallies, cool return, precise serves. And throughout, he never smiled, never spoke, never changed the expression on his face.

Jimmy took the first set, 6–4, but his attacking strategy backfired in the second set. Borg continued staying back at the baseline, letting Jimmy walk into his own destruction. It was as if Connors couldn't wait to set up winners. He was rushing his shots, particularly forehands, and it cost him the set, 3–6.

When they started the third set, it was anybody's match. Jimmy looked annoyed at himself—which could be either good or bad, depending on how it affected him. As he served to open the first game, it didn't look at all good for Jimmy, Borg, the inscrutable tennis machine, took the first point, then the next, and the next. Jimmy, shaking his head, set to serve. He bounced the ball four times, lofted it, and sent it humming at Borg. But Borg was ready and sent it back easily. Jimmy lunged, ramming it back over the net—but too far. The game went to Borg, breaking Jimmy's serve.

When Borg began his serve, Connors' rooters felt deep concern. And they had good cause to—the Swede was killing the American. And then, down at break point, Jimmy unleashed a backhander—his bread-and-butter shot—deep into the Swede's forehand corner. Bjorn scampered after it, but he slipped and went rolling over the ground as the ball blurred by. When he stood, his shirt was smeared with gray-green clay dust. The dirt was nothing, however. Borg had also cut open his right knee, and it was bleeding. He studied his leg for a moment, then took a few tentative steps to test it. He was shaken but, after receiving medical attention, said he was ready to resume play.

Even though his outward response was exactly the same as always—no expression—Borg seemed to lose his grip on his game. Jimmy went ahead, gaining confidence as he stopped his impatient rushing to get in winners. The crowd, quiet as each point was played, applauded both competitors. This was tennis at its height, and everyone knew it.

The third set was a long one, with the lead switching from Borg to Connors and then, almost too late, back to Borg. Then it was 6–6, with a tie breaker needed to decide the set. And what a tie breaker it was! The first point, on Jimmy's serve, was his on a sharply angled backhand volley placement. Borg sent over a serve loaded with topspin. Jimmy miscalculated, and the score was tied, 1–1. Jimmy took the next one when Bjorn overplayed a forehand shot, but the score went to 2–2 when Connors double-faulted on his serve. There was no fault on his next serve, but it didn't matter as he dropped the point on a backhand that traveled too far. And Bjorn snared the next point, on his own serve, upping his lead to 4–2. Then, still serving, the Swedish iceberg overplayed a forehand, making it 4–3.

Jimmy tied it up, only to lose the next two points. It was 6–4, and Borg was serving at set point. Both his serve and Jimmy's return were good, and the rallying began. Both players played it safe, waiting for the other guy to make a mistake. Borg was the one to make it, and the score was 6–5. Still set point for Bjorn, with Connors serving. Again the careful shots, and again the point went to Jimmy, 6–6. Breathing more easily, Jimmy set to serve. He squinted across the net in the fading light, then spiked a blazer that ignited the fans. Jimmy had aced Bjorn: 7–6!

This was the kind of clutch play made by true champions, and the crowd showed they knew by shattering the air with their applause. In that instant something special had happened: The hostility which had been dogging Jimmy for years simply evaporated. It was as if the explosiveness of the ace under pressure and the equally explosive reaction of the crowd had, at the same time, destroyed the past and made the future *now*.

But Borg hadn't joined Jimmy's fans. He came back on his two serves to even the score and to take the lead at 8–7. For the third time he had Jimmy at set point. This time Jimmy launched an overhead shot that had tennis nuts whistling in amazement. It was 8–8 . . . until a long forehand stroke put it at 9–8, Borg's favor. Set point number four against Jimmy. Could he do it one more time?

The stadium lights blazed on. It was getting late, and the temperature was dropping; but nobody even thought of leaving. Borg served, Connors returned it solidly, and Borg, moving in, sent over a two-handed backhand. Jimmy jumped on it. Using an overhead like the one that had pulled it out for him a few minutes earlier, he evened the score at 9–9. The next point, another winner from Jimmy's bag of magic tricks, was a two-fisted crosscourter that caught Borg out of position: 10–9, Connors. The 16,000 people in the stands sounded like 60,000 as they cheered and whistled for Jimmy.

He had Borg at set point now. Connors served and moved in. Borg returned service, and Jimmy reached for it, sending a spinner across the net. Borg lunged and drove a hard backhander toward the corner—but too wide. Connors had the tie breaker, 11–9, and the third set, 7–6. The thriller had taken one hour and ten minutes—seventy minutes nobody would ever forget.

Jimmy played with the rhythm of a clock in the fourth set, taking the score to 5–4 without too many problems. Then, at 40–30, he served for match point. As Jimmy said later, "I just wanted to get to the net and say, 'Pass me.' " Unfortunately Borg did, and the score was deuce. Jimmy won the next point, giving him the advantage, which he again failed to follow up on. Back to deuce. But the next time Jimmy got the advantage he kept it, winning the game, the set (6–4), and the 1976 U.S. Open Championship. The three-hour, ten-minute slugfest was over. Jimmy stood on the court as the fans rose in a circle and applauded. He stood there for at least five seconds, not realizing it was over, not understanding that the cheering was for him. And then it hit him, and he grinned like a little kid.

Afterward, with the thrill of it all still flushing his face, Jimmy said, "We killed each other out there. Since Forest Hills changed to clay and I'm not supposed to be a clay-court player, it was *very* satisfying."

"It was everything anyone could have asked for," wrote Neil Amdur in the New York *Times*. "And more. Courage and greatness flowed across the stadium of the West Side Tennis Club."

For Jimmy, courageous and great, it was more than just another important win. It marked the moment at which he moved away from boyhood into manhood and into his rightful place as the number one tennis player of the 1970s. And maybe, as some have said, the greatest ever. For there were many more years left to his career, many more exciting wins for Jimmy Connors, king of the courts.

Index

Aaron, Hank, 120
Addison, Terry, 57
Ali, Muhammad, 54, 92
Althoff Catholic High School, 38
Amdur, Neil, 155
Amritraj, Vijay, 118, 146
Ashe, Arthur, 60, 66, 100-2, 140-41, 147
Assumption Catholic High School, 35-37
Astrodome, 127
Australian Open Tournament, 119-26, 137

Baltimore Indoor Championship, 69, 96
Bassett, Coach (UCLA), 61
Belleville, Illinois, 15, 36-38, 43, 61, 91, 93
Berra, Dale, 27
Berra, Larry, 27
Berra, Yogi, 27
Beverly Hills Tennis Club, 45-51
Birmingham International Indoor Tournament, 129
Borg, Bjorn, 104-5, 141, 148, 150-55
Borowiak, Jeff, 64, 108-9
Buchholtz, Butch, 32-33
Buckeye Tournament, 100

Caesar's Palace, 126, 131, 137
Carmichael, Bob, 57
Carson, Johnny, 132
CBS, 138-39
Chamberlain, Wilt, 51
Connors, Gloria, 15, 25-26, 28-38, 40, 43-48, 52, 60-61, 69, 74, 77, 79, 97, 102, 119

Connors, James Scott, Jr.,
    childhood, 25-35
    dating, 61, 75-78, 93-97, 136
    engagement to Chris Evert, 16-17, 24, 102-4, 119, 136
    first tournament victory, 34
    playing style, 17, 21-22, 25, 32-34, 47-50, 52-53, 67, 98-99, 120
    religion, 38, 94
    teenage life, 35-50, 61-63
    turning pro, 35-36, 68-70
Connors, James, Sr., 30, 33, 40, 45, 61
Connors, John, 25-26, 28-30, 35
Cooper, John, 97
Cornejo, Patricio, 59
Cox, Mark, 129
Crookenden, Ian, 132

Davis Cup
    junior team, 55
    team, 71-72, 128-29, 134, 142-43
Dell, Donald, 71
Dent, Phil, 14, 146
Denver, Colo., 138-39
Dibbs, Eddie, 141
Dibley, Colin, 146
DiMaggio, Joe, 92
Dunlop (tennis balls), 130

East St. Louis, 25, 29-30, 35
Eastern Grass Court Championship, 105-6
Eastwood, Clint, 132
Elizabeth II, 14
Emerson, Roy, 55, 129
Evert, Chris, 15-17, 24, 27, 75-78,

93-97, 99, 102-4, 106-7, 119, 136
Evert, Colette, 77, 97
Evert, Jim, 27, 93

Fillol, Jaime, 59
Fleming, Peter, 147
Forest Hills, see U.S. Nationals
Forest Park, Illinois, 35
Fort Lauderdale, Florida, 39, 93-94, 96, 103
Fraser, Neale, 97
Frazier, Joe, 17
French Open Tournament, 128

Gerulaitis, Vitas, 132, 148
Gonzales, Richard (Pancho), 51-55, 57-59, 65, 67, 76, 107, 131
Gorman, Tom, 71, 92
Gottfried, Brian, 39, 139, 148
Graebner, Clark, 96

Haggars Co., 138
Heldman, Gladys, 27
Heldman, Julie, 27
Heston, Charlton, 132
Hewitt, Bob, 79-90, 92, 146
Holiday Park, 93
Howe, Gordie, 27

Illinois State High School Tournament, 36

Jacksonville, Florida, 69

Kalamazoo, Michigan, 41, 43
Kent, Duke of, 14, 23
Keeler, Willie, 82
King, Alan, 132
King, Billie Jean, 92, 97, 127-28
Kodes, Jan, 15, 109-10, 148-49
Kramer, Jack, 126

La Costa, California, 129
Las Vegas, Nevada, 12, 126, 129-31, 137-39
Laver, Rod, 12, 117-19, 126, 128-34, 137-39
Longwood Cricket Club, see U.S. Pro Championship
Lutz, Bob, 60

McKinley, Chuck, 35-36
McManus, Jim, 55
McNair, Fred, 148

Madison Square Garden, 118
Maravich, Pete, 27
Maravich, Press, 27
Martin, Dino, 62
Mayer, Alex, Jr., 41, 96
Metreveli, Alex, 97, 106, 109
Moore, Ray, 55, 99
Mount Washington, New Hampshire, 118

Nastase, Ilie, 57, 69, 90-91, 97, 111, 113-14, 127, 147, 150
National Collegiate Association of America (NCAA) Championship, 60, 63-67
National Claycourt Championship, 104-5
Junior, 55
National Hardcourt Championship, Junior, 55
National Outdoor Championship, Junior, 55
NBC, 138
New York Times, 155
Newcombe, John, 101, 119-24, 127, 137-40

Okker, Tom, 57, 100, 117
Orantes, Manuel, 141, 146, 148

Pacific Southwest Tournament, 55, 100-1
Paish, John, 76-77
Panatta, Adriano, 147
Pasarell, Charles, 60, 100

Queen's Cup Tournament, The, 74-77, 79

Rahim, Haroon, 63
Ralston, Dennis, 60, 71, 142
Ramirez, Raul, 147
Rexford High School, 45-47
Richey, Cliff, 99
Riessen, Marty, 57, 116-17
Riggs, Bobby, 127
Riordan, Bill, 15, 70-71, 73-74, 77, 97, 107, 110, 118, 130, 137
Roche, Tony, 120
"Rocket", see Laver, Rod
Rose, Pete, 27
Rosewall, Ken, 13-14, 17-24, 112-14, 116, 149

Rote, Kyle, Sr., 27
Rote, Kyle, Jr., 27
Rothman's International Tournament, 101
Ruth, Babe, 66
Ryan, Dick, 35-37
Ryan, Nolan, 58

St. Louis, Missouri, 32, 34
St. Louis Armory, 34
St. Philip School, 29, 35
Segura, Francisco (Pancho), 21-22, 24, 44-50, 51-52, 54, 65, 67, 74, 82, 107, 129, 149
Segura, Spencer, 45, 47, 61, 119
Smith, Stan, 19, 60, 66, 71, 76, 79, 99, 101-2, 117, 148
Solomon Harold, 141, 146
South African Open Tournament, 101-2
South Bend, Indiana, 63
Southern California Tournament, 55
Southern Illinois Tournament, 34
Spander, Art, 135
Sporting News, The, 135
Stanford University, 63
Stockton, Dick, 15-17, 43, 99
Swedish Open Tournament, 101

Tanner, Roscoe, 43, 63-66, 111-12, 144
Thompson, Bertha, 26, 28-31, 33-34, 37, 45-46, 60-61, 71-73, 77, 134
Thunderbird Tournament, 55
Trabert, Tony, 142
Triple A Invitational Tournament, 35-36
"Two Moms," see Thompson, Bertha

UCLA, 60-61, 63-64, 67-68
United States Lawn Tennis Association (USLTA, later USTA), 37, 60, 63, 68, 70, 128, 142
U S. Nationals, 53, 55-59, 67, 92-93, 100, 104-16, 118-19, 141-42, 145-55
U.S. Pro Championships, 99-100, 101, 150

Van Dillen, Erik, 71, 143, 147
Vilas, Guillermo, 141, 149-50

West Side Tennis Club, 55, 74
Williams, Andy, 132
Wilson (tennis balls), 130
Wimbledon, 13-24, 73, 78-91, 92, 97, 102-4, 106, 109-12, 114-15, 118, 133, 136-37, 140-41, 144, 150
Woods, W. Harcourt, 71
World Championship Tennis (WCT), 70-71, 73, 99, 137-38, 150
World Team Tennis, 127-28

The Author

Francene Sabin is the author of the recent well-received *Set Point: The Story of Chris Evert* from Putnam's. She is a prolific author, sometimes writing on her own and sometimes in collaboration with her husband, Louis. Together they are the authors of a longtime bestselling book from Putnam's, *Dogs of America*. The Sabins and their son live in Milltown, New Jersey.